Uncovering Gold

Romancing the Californian Cowboys

Book 3

S M SPENCER

Cover design by BookPOD

Cover images by iStockphoto

eISBN: 978-1-922270-55-9

ISBN: 978-1-922270-70-2 (pbk)

Related books in the Copperhead Creek Australian Romance series:

A Chance to Come True

A Chance to Get it Right

A Chance to Let Go

A Chance to Belong

A Chance for Snow

Related books in the Copperhead Creek Mystery series:

Murder at the Creek

Related books in the Romancing the Californian Cowboys series:

Discovering Gold

Striking Gold

As a teen, my mother introduced me to the world of romantic suspense through the books of incredible authors like Daphne du Maurier and Mary Stewart. If not for the enjoyment I got from those books, I doubt I'd have been tempted to try my own hand at writing.

I want to thank my mother for starting me on this journey, and the others who have helped me to continue along this path.

PROLOGUE

Assistance Sought in Locating Missing Masons Flat Woman

Page 3, The Goldfields Tribune

March 5th, 1985

Local authorities are seeking information as to the whereabouts of missing Masons Flat woman, Evelyn Harrison. Mrs Harrison was last seen while working at the family butcher shop in Main Street, Masons Flat on Friday, January 11th of this year. The shop closed at approximately five o'clock, so she might have been seen driving home or elsewhere early that evening or in the following days.

Mrs Harrison drives a white 1982 Ford Escort. She is 29 years old, five foot seven, of slim build, and has long dark hair and brown eyes.

Anyone with information relating to her possible whereabouts at any time since her disappearance is asked to contact us on the numbers listed below.

CHAPTER 1

Present Day

Taylor Mason stood in her newly acquired shop's vacant interior, finding it hard to believe it was actually hers. She'd done it. She'd bought the building that would soon become her very own bakery. She truly belonged in Masons Flat, California now—the town named after her ancestors—and the place she'd grown to love over a six-week stay with her sister at Christmas.

Even though she'd seen it from the outside on that visit, this was the first time she'd been inside the shop, having purchased it remotely from her home in Australia. She'd relied on the photos to make the purchase decision, and could now see first-hand what a few friends had tried to tell her: nothing ever looks quite the same in reality as it does in the photos used by realtors.

Seeing it now, it was obvious the shop had been deserted for many years. Dust covered every flat surface, the floorboards squeaked and were filthy, and the walls, though they sported a few clean patches where shelves must have protected the pale green paint, were faded and grubby. She couldn't help but wonder if the photos might have been taken right after the last tenants had vacated the shop.

She stood there for a few moments, taking in the feel of the front of the shop—what would be the retail area. Of the two large floor-to-ceiling windows, one faced roughly east, and would overlook the Gold Nugget Saloon once the boards over the window were removed. The other, at the front of the shop, faced south. Light might have just managed to come through the years of grime on that window but for the remains of the painted sign incorrectly advising prospective customers that this was Masons Flat Butchers.

Taylor's mind swam with ideas for new signage for the Masons Flat Bakery, and she couldn't wait to get started on the designs.

When she'd thoroughly investigated the front area, she ventured to the back of the shop, which represented about two-thirds of the building. Here she found a small office and washroom on one side and a large, industrial double sink on the other. The middle of this back area was empty, all the tables and appliances long since gone, with marks on the floor being the only indication of where the tables had been. One relatively new light fitting remained intact inside the small office, but the ones in the larger area hung precariously on wires that looked to be as old as the hills.

In contrast to the front of the shop, with its large windows which would eventually allow natural light to flood through, this back area sported only highlight windows—ones designed not to allow passers-by to see inside. The area also smelled surprisingly musty, considering the August air was hot and dry.

After a few minutes, she returned to the front and opened the door, but it had an automatic closure devise on it and wouldn't stay open. She peered around the dingy space until she noticed an old rubber doorstop, then propped the front door open, allowing fresh air to flow and the musty smell to clear.

It didn't take a genius to work out why no one had wanted to lease the property. The entire shop needed a remodel—one that could easily run to tens of thousands of dollars, if not more. Possibly much more, if the old building needed to be re-stumped and re-wired.

But it didn't matter.

Not one bit.

This was her shop now—hers to do with as she saw fit. She would turn it into the bakery of her dreams—and she wouldn't even have to ask permission or seek agreement from anyone as to the appearance, layout or cost. And since she'd bought it outright, there wasn't even a mortgage holder to question her decisions.

If someone had told her a year ago that she would be selling her house in Melbourne and moving to a small town at the base of the Sierra Nevada Mountain Range in California, where she'd be opening a bakery, and that both of her sisters would also be living in California, she'd have said they were nuts.

And yet, that's exactly what was happening.

And, thanks to the house Uncle Steven had left to her, Alex and Casey, she had somewhere to live rent free as well.

She looked up and sighed, feeling a tentative smile cross her lips as she whispered a thank you to her great-uncle and grandfather. She couldn't remember meeting either of the men, yet she owed them a huge debt of gratitude for the inheritance they'd left to her and her sisters—one substantial enough that if they didn't do anything foolish, none of them should have to worry about money ever again.

As she headed to the back again to check out what would eventually be her office, the sound of footsteps approaching along the wooden walkway caught her attention. She turned toward the door, hopeful as to the identity of the visitor.

'Denver,' she said with a smile in her voice. 'Geez, you're a sight for sore eyes.'

With his dark hair and eyes, Denver, the younger brother of her soon-to-be brother-in-law, was as much a chip-off-the-block of his brother Travis, as she was of her older sister Alex, with her long auburn locks and gold-flecked emerald green eyes. But it wasn't Denver's looks attracting her to him; he had to be one of the nicest men, if not *the* nicest man, she'd ever met.

He returned her smile enthusiastically as he stepped inside. 'As are you. I've been looking forward to seeing you ever since Alex said you were coming back. I hope you're ready for a rematch at the pool table.' A mischievous grin snuck onto his face, and his eyes fairly twinkled.

'Oh, absolutely, I can't wait for a game. I never did find anywhere at home to play. Of course, not having you as an opponent took away a bit of the incentive for me to look.'

His mischievous grin turned to a shy smile at her not-so-subtle compliment.

'Aw, shucks, Taylor. Does that mean you might possibly have missed me as much as I've missed you?' he asked, his tone playful.

She walked up and threw her arms around him for a big hug. As his strong arms wrapped around her, a sense of homecoming washed over her.

After a few moments, she loosened her arms and stepped back, matching his smile with another warm one of her own. Already indescribably happy about the shop and about being back in California, reuniting with Denver Gold—the sort of man she'd often wished she could have met in Melbourne—made everything seem too good to believe.

She hadn't been sure how she'd feel when she first saw him. After all, as close as they'd become over the six weeks she'd been in town for the Christmas holidays, their relationship hadn't been a physical one—perhaps because they'd both known their time together was limited, or perhaps because they were destined to simply be good friends. And while she'd enjoyed every minute of the time they'd spent together, which had been extensive given he'd had a leg in plaster at the time and couldn't do much work around his property, they hadn't kept in touch after she'd gone home.

'Geez, it's good to see you,' she repeated, not quite answering his question. 'And how's the leg? Not giving you any more strife?'

'None at all. I started doing most of my regular chores not long after you left, and then once we got into spring I started riding again and I haven't looked back since.'

'That's great to hear.'

'And how was the trip over? I nearly dropped around to see you last night, but I figured you'd be exhausted after the long flight.'

'I slept quite a bit on the plane, actually. Alex took me to the grocery store on the way home to get the essentials, and then all I did was unpack my two bags, take a long shower and crash in front of the television.'

'Did you bring much with you?'

'Just what I could fit in two suitcases. I've got a small container coming over by boat with the rest of my things.'

He nodded. 'Guess you don't need a hand, then?'

'Not at home, thanks, but I could use a hand here. Do you think you could recommend someone to help me with all this?' she asked, waving her arms around to indicate the whole of the shop.

According to everyone in town, Denver was the best carpenter for miles. But, given how busy she knew he was with his ranch, she didn't expect him to actually do the work. However, if he could point her to the second-best carpenter it would save her a lot of time.

Denver cocked his head, looking around. 'I think I might have time to supervise a couple of guys to do the work for you. Just how much are you thinking of changing?'

Taylor scrunched her face into a grimace. 'All of it? I mean, the location of the main walls is okay—separating what will be the retail, office and work areas—but the walls and floors look awful. And of course I'll need to purchase refrigeration and counters and ovens and stainless-steel tables and display cabinets and, well, you know, everything.'

Denver nodded, his lips pursed. 'It won't be hard if you're happy with the location of the walls. Most of the rest is nothing much more than paint and plaster. These old buildings were made to last so hopefully there won't be any structural works required. And as for getting the right equipment, I've definitely got some good contacts.'

She looked up at the light fittings. 'And a good electrician? I suspect there could be a lot of extra standards for commercial kitchens?'

'Again, that won't be hard. I know just the guy—he does this sort of thing all the time.'

'Awesome. And, I hope I don't sound too pushy or anything, but how soon do you think we can get started?'

Denver cocked a brow. 'Wow, you've been in town for, what, twenty-four hours? And you want to get started straight away?' he asked, a chuckle punctuating his words.

She threw her head back with a gentle laugh. 'You're right. I've only just arrived, but wouldn't it be wonderful to have the bakery open before Christmas? I mean, I have no idea how long all this will take, but Christmas is only four months away.'

Still smiling, he threw his arms around her and pulled her toward him in another bear-hug. 'It's so good to have you back,' he said, squeezing her tight.

When he released her, she stepped back, allowing an eyebrow to arch inquisitively.

He shook his head slowly as he continued. 'Yeah, okay, I'll get onto a couple of guys this afternoon. I won't let you down.'

~~*~~

At five minutes to seven, Taylor heard a car pull up at the front of her house. She didn't have to peek out the window to know it would be her sister, Alex, with her fiancé, Travis, but she looked anyway. Sure enough, the familiar Range Rover was stopped in the driveway with Travis at the wheel, her sister beside him, and she could just make out Denver in the back.

They were off to have dinner at the Masons Hotel, to welcome her back to California. Her twin sister, Casey, would join them along with her partner, Nick, who just happened to be Travis' and Denver's cousin.

The absurdity of three sisters successfully dating two brothers and a cousin wasn't lost on her, and was a lot of the reason she'd been coy about answering Denver's question as to whether she'd missed him. The thought of them dating seemed destined to end in disaster.

Taylor climbed into the back beside Denver, fastened her seatbelt, and then turned and smiled at him. He grinned as he reached over and took her hand to give it a gentle squeeze. His touch warmed her to the core—as nice as any touch she'd ever experienced—but she still wanted to be cautious. She squeezed back, then pulled her hand away and disguised her reasons for doing so by leaning forward to chat to Alex in the front seat.

It was only a few minutes into town and, when they made their way into the hotel, Casey and Nick were already seated in the dining room.

'Welcome home,' Casey said, racing over to give her twin a big hug.

Taylor had missed her sister over the past five months—the longest they'd ever been separated. Seeing her again completed the sense of homecoming. 'You look good, Case. Guess Sacramento is treating you well. And of course, you've been in summer.' She looked down at her own arms, white by comparison to the golden skin she could see between Casey's tattoos.

'Have to say, everything is going better than I'd dared dream,' she said, turning and smiling at Nick. 'Even my new job is terrific, and my new boss is grooming me to be second in charge.'

'That's fabulous. I'm so happy for you. And Nick,' she said, turning to her sister's boyfriend, 'it's good to see you, too. You look happy.'

He pulled her forward for a hug as well. 'I am happy,' he said with a broad smile as he released her. 'With Casey by my side, what's not to be happy about?'

When all the greetings were done, the group settled at the table. While they were waiting for their meals to arrive, the conversation turned to Taylor's bakery endeavour. Alex asked her to describe her plans, and Taylor obliged enthusiastically.

Travis cocked his head, and squinted as he turned to Denver. 'How much of your time do you think this project is going to take up?'

'Don't worry, Trav. I've already spoken to a couple of guys who will do most of the work. I'll supervise, but it should just be a matter of checking in from time to time.'

'Good. I mean, I'm glad you can help with it, but I'd hate to have to drag Nick back up here to help me with the horses again,' Travis said, his voice carrying a slight hint of laughter.

Denver shook his head. 'Don't stress. It'll just be a bit of my time doing some of the planning, and ordering equipment ... that sort of thing.'

By quarter to nine, Taylor started to nod off at the table so the group said their goodbyes. When Travis pulled into her driveway, Denver quickly jumped out and came around to walk her to her front door.

As she dug down to the bottom of her purse for the house keys, her mind raced. Denver stood right beside her, watching her every move. And Travis and Alex were in the car, with a prime view. Should she kiss him goodnight?

When she finally got the front door open, she turned to face him. 'Thank you for agreeing to help me get the bakery remodelled. If I had to do it all myself, it'd be weeks before I got as much done as you did in one afternoon.'

'Hey, give yourself a bit more credit. A few days maybe ... or a week,' he said with a chuckle. 'But seriously, there's no need to thank me every time you see me. Giving you a hand will be my pleasure. Besides, it'll give me an excuse to see you more often than just over the pool table.'

She could feel herself blushing, grateful for the darkness. 'Oh, I can't wait to have a game. When do you want to play?' She didn't want to come across as trying to monopolise his time, and yet the thought of a night out playing pool sounded terrific.

He reached up and put his hands on her shoulders, then leaned forward and kissed her forehead.

‘I’ve got nothing planned tomorrow night. Let’s see how quickly you get over your jetlag. If you’re up for it tomorrow, that’s fine by me.’

She watched as he turned to make his way back to the car. Things were perfect, really. And not just for her, but for her sisters as well. She was so glad Alex had met Travis, and that his brother and cousin had both turned out to be so nice.

Once again, she looked up and said a silent thank you to her great-uncle and grandfather, and then went inside and locked the door behind her.

CHAPTER 2

1984 – Eve

This was my first trip back to San Francisco since I'd stopped working in the city over two years earlier. The familiar scent hit me as I approached the Bay Bridge with my windows wide open—the sharp salty tang of the bay mixed with the fumes from the surrounding cars, trucks and busses. It was a strange thing to miss, and yet I now realised I had missed it terribly.

The traffic on the bridge was chaotic, but from memory, it always was no matter what the time of day. A pang of regret crept over me, regret that it had been so long since I'd made this trip.

Some days I found it hard to believe I'd allowed myself to be convinced to give up my lucrative job with a major San Francisco accounting firm—the one I'd worked so hard to qualify for. Now, as I thought about my choice, Don's voice echoed in my mind and I replayed the conversation that brought my career to an end—the conversation that turned me from a career woman to a small-town wife and bookkeeper.

'I can't keep doing this long-distance relationship, sweetheart,' he'd said, his eyes imploring me to stay with him, and his hand softly rubbing my arm as I threw my overnight suitcase onto the backseat of my car. 'I want to have you here with me every day and every night. I want us to be a family, and to have a family. Marry me? I'll make you happy, I promise.' And then he'd dropped to one knee and pulled a small box from his pocket.

The ring, simple yet stunning, had fit perfectly. But why wouldn't it have? My father would have helped him with the size. Dad's subtle hints about wanting grandchildren, as well as how much he hated having to do the bookwork for the family business, hadn't fallen on deaf ears. I'd heard him—every time.

In the end, I'd given in to both of the men in my life, and within a few months I'd become a dutiful wife and daughter, making them both so proud. Exactly as they'd wanted. And at the time, I suppose I'd convinced myself it was what I'd wanted, too.

Even so, the niggling sense of doubt that persisted had grown, and the importance of keeping up my Continuing Education credits had become more and more apparent. I was a Certified Public Accountant after all. Not only something to be proud of, but something I could fall back on if small town life eventually got to us—or to me.

It had taken numerous discussions with Don to get him to accept that keeping up my credentials would be a great benefit for us, and eventually he agreed with the idea. And so today, I'd left Masons Flat well before sunrise to get to the city on time for a two-day conference.

After a quick coffee and an egg and bacon sandwich in the hotel's café, I headed to the conference room. As one of the first to arrive, I chose a seat with a clear view of the lectern and overhead screen, on the end of a row, well positioned so if I needed to get up during the presentations I could do so without disturbing others.

It wasn't long before the crowds arrived and the noise level in the room rose. I had to continually get up to allow people into the middle seats, but I didn't mind. Once the row was mostly filled, I pulled out a notebook and pen and sat in anticipation of a full day of learning about the latest changes to accounting standards.

As the lecturer made his way onto the stage, one last attendee came and stood next to me. He was about a foot away from me, but even so my whole body seemed drawn to him, like a paperclip to a magnet.

'Excuse me,' he said, leaning down toward me to speak in a voice as warm as honey. 'Is the seat beside you taken?'

I looked up into a pair of hazel-green eyes, positively glowing against his warm brown skin.

'Oh, no, it isn't,' I stuttered, standing to allow him to pass.

As he moved past me, I caught a whiff of fresh bath soap, suggesting he'd possibly stayed in the hotel overnight and had showered only minutes ago.

I'd met lots of men in college—men from all over the world, in actual fact—but not one had ever had such an impact upon me as this man did right now.

Without effort.

Without intention.

And, most likely, without his knowledge.

As the lecturer proceeded, I tried my best to focus on his words, squinting to pick up the smallest details on his slide presentation in order to take notes. I tried all kinds of tricks to force myself to pay attention, challenging myself to write down everything on his slides. Yet as hard as I tried, I couldn't shake the sense of being drawn to this intriguing green-eyed stranger.

When the morning session concluded, I stood and set my notebook down on the seat. The stranger beside me stood as well, doing the same. Then he caught my eye.

'Well, that had to have been one of the driest presentations I've ever heard at these sessions,' he said, raising a brow. 'Did you find it as bad as I did, or is it just me?'

'I've never been to one of these before,' I replied honestly. 'This is my first since I stopped working in the city.'

When I hadn't moved, he reached out and placed a hand on my arm. 'The people in the middle need out ... shall we?' he asked, nodding toward the tables set up with coffee and snacks.

'Oh, of course. Sorry,' I said, looking past him at the others. I stepped away, with him right beside me, and made my way toward the food and drink tables.

'I'm Andrew,' he said as we joined the line of people waiting to be served. He pointed to his name tag, pinned to his shirt. Andrew Fletcher.

I looked up and met his intense gaze once again. It nearly floored me. 'Eve. Well, Evelyn actually, but I prefer being called Eve.' My tag read Evelyn Gold. I'd married Don after I'd become a CPA, and had never bothered to change my professional name. It was quite common, women using their maiden names in business, or at least that's what I'd told Don when he'd asked about it.

'Eve it shall be, then,' he said in his honey smooth voice.

The sensation that filled me was something I hadn't experienced before. It might have been recklessness, or perhaps just a desire for adventure. I wasn't sure how to define it, or if I even wanted to. It simply wasn't anything I'd felt before. And yet I knew, deep inside, where this sensation would lead.

Not once in my four years at college, nor in the three years I worked at the accounting firm, had I even considered cheating on Don. Not even before we were engaged. And yet, I knew this was different. All it would take was for him to give me the slightest encouragement. Did he feel it too? Was that why he was looking at me with such intensity? Why he'd assumed I'd join him for coffee at the break? Or was I just so caught up in my own feelings it hadn't occurred to me he might have this effect on every woman he meets?

Once we had our coffee and had each selected a muffin, we moved to the side of the room away from the large group of people.

He looked around for a moment before turning back to me. 'I don't know a soul here. Do you?'

I glanced around, wondering if any of my former colleagues might be in attendance, but then again, the firm usually conducted its own in-house training sessions so it wasn't likely.

'I don't think so,' I answered, surprised at the breathless sound of my voice.

'Are you staying at the hotel? I don't mean to be nosy, just wondering if you're here for both days.'

'Yes,' I replied, glad he'd asked. 'I'm staying upstairs. It's nearly a two-hour drive from my place to get here, so I'll stay tonight and then drive home after tomorrow's session.'

'Me too. I live in Santa Cruz. It's not quite two hours, but nearly. I could have driven home tonight, but I left plenty of food out for the cats and decided not to push my luck with drinking and driving. There are always drinks after these things, you know? So ... maybe we should have dinner together? Of course, only if you haven't already made plans?'

'No, I don't have any plans. I figured they'd serve some food after the last session, or else I'd get room service. I'm not too adventurous when I'm on my own.' And walking around the city at night alone was the one thing I'd promised Don I wouldn't do. I'd never said I wouldn't have dinner with another attendee.

'Good. I know a great Chinese restaurant not far from here. I don't know about you, but just thinking about a bowl of hot and sour soup is making my mouth water.'

'It's one of my favourites, too. That's one of the things I miss the most about no longer working in the city—all the interesting food. In ...' I hesitated, quickly concluding it would be best not to mention where I lived, 'the town where I live, we don't have any interesting restaurants.'

'Chinese it is, then. We can arrange a time at the end of the day,' he said with a nod.

'Okay, that sounds good.'

A bell sounded, signalling the start of the next session, but as we made our way back to our seats, all I could think about was that we'd be having dinner together.

A part of me felt wicked. And although I knew I shouldn't be making these plans, the excitement far outweighed any sense of wrongdoing.

CHAPTER 3

Present Day

Taylor leaned over the pool table, checking the angle to the pocket. She hadn't played in months, but it looked to be an easy enough shot. The table was pretty open for one thing, given Denver had pocketed five balls on his first turn.

She took a deep breath, lined up, and gave the cue ball a clean whack. When her ball went into the correct pocket she practically jumped with joy.

'I haven't lost it,' she said, turning toward Denver, who stood leaning up against the wall behind her.

'You certainly haven't,' Denver replied, his brow creeping up provocatively.

'Loser buys the next round,' she said with a wink.

She hit another ball, but this second one wasn't quite as co-operative, and bounced back toward the middle of the table.

'Bad luck,' Denver said as he walked up to take his turn.

'So, these guys you've lined up ... you said they're okay to start tomorrow morning?'

Denver cocked his head as he prepared to take his shot. 'Are you trying to distract me so I'll miss?'

'Who me? Never,' she replied with feigned innocence.

'Let's finish this game, then you can buy me another drink and we can talk about the work.'

And just like that, Denver cleared the rest of the balls. They handed the table to a couple of guys who'd been waiting nearby, then made their way to the bar.

'What can I get ya?' Darleen asked as she approached with her hands on her hips. Darleen had turned into a good friend of Taylor's when they'd spent many an hour baking together the previous December. She'd also recently taken over the saloon—a gift from Taylor and her sisters upon learning she was a distant relative of theirs.

'Two of your finest,' Taylor said, pulling some money from her pocket. 'I lost, so it's my shout.'

'Coming right up,' Darleen said, filling two tall glasses with the amber liquid and sliding them across the bar.

'Cheers,' Taylor said, tapping her glass against Denver's.

'Cheers,' Denver said before taking a long sip of the beer, and wiping the back of his hand across his mouth.

As she watched his hand touch his lips, thoughts of what it would be like to kiss him crossed her mind. She realised she'd been staring when she turned her head slightly and caught the look on Darleen's face—a look accompanied by a raised eyebrow. Taylor swallowed, rolling her eyes briefly, but Darleen just grinned and walked off to serve another customer.

Luckily, Denver appeared oblivious to the entire exchange.

'So, I'll meet the guys at the shop at nine. Grant Davies is sort of a general handyman,' Denver said, 'and Jeff Abbott is the electrician. We were lucky to grab Jeff with such short notice, because another job of his got delayed. Grant will start with the windows, and then as Jeff finishes off sections of the electrical work, Grant will come along behind him and do all the plastering and painting. Oh, and Grant says he's had a bit of experience with flooring, so I may get him to look at that too. Could save us from having to get someone else in to do the floors, depending on what you want done.'

'That's wonderful. I can hardly believe it's all happening so fast,' Taylor said with a shiver.

'It wouldn't be if you'd wanted to change all the walls around—we'd have needed permits for that. We'll have a look at the foundations tomorrow, but nothing I've seen so far suggests there are any structural issues, so I think we'll be able to press on pretty quickly.'

'Fabulous. I had a look at the website you suggested and everything I'll need is there, but it says six to twelve weeks for the ovens. That's too long.'

Denver shook his head. 'Let me make a few calls tomorrow and see if I can get them somewhere else then. They're not the only supplier around here.'

'I don't want to take up any more of your time than necessary,' Taylor replied, conscious of Denver's workloads at his ranch.

'Don't worry about that—it won't take long. So ... I was thinking we might have dinner Saturday night. If you're free?'

'Dinner? Yes, I certainly am free. At the hotel?' Warmth penetrated her at the thought of having a real date with him.

Denver gave her a crooked smile. 'Um, no, not at the hotel. There's a rockabilly band playing over in Sonora, so I thought we might have a quick dinner there in town and then go dancing afterwards.'

Her eyes grew wide at the prospect. She'd heard stories about what a good dancer Denver was, but hadn't seen any evidence of it. She'd always wanted to learn swing dancing, and he could be just the one to teach her. 'That sounds wonderful.'

Denver sighed, then picked up his glass and skulled the last of his beer. 'Want another?' he asked. 'Or are you ready for a re-match?'

~~*~~

Taylor arrived at the shop a quarter-hour early, propped the front door open and then had another good look around. The musty smell had all but dissipated—perhaps it had just been stale air from the place being locked up for so long.

She closed her eyes, imagining it all freshly painted, with display cabinets and racks filled with bread and scrolls and meat pies and Cornish pasties. Oh, and all the desserts she planned to do—everything from individual-sized pies to slices and cupcakes. And brownies. One thing she'd learned was that Americans loved their brownies. Her mouth began to water, just thinking about all the tempting delicacies she'd create.

The sound of footsteps approaching told her Denver, too, had arrived early. Only when she turned, it wasn't Denver.

The man who stood at the doorway had to be taller than Denver, and by the look of his shoulders he no doubt spent a fair amount of time at a gym. He had light brown hair, dark brown eyes, and looked as though he hadn't shaved for several days. He was definitely attractive, but it wasn't just his physical appearance grabbing her attention. It was as though when he'd entered the room he'd sucked up all the oxygen, leaving her breathless.

'You must be the owner of the shop,' he said in a deep and raspy voice as he removed his ear-buds and flicked off his music.

'Yes, I'm Taylor,' she said. Her voice sounding less breathless than she'd feared. 'And you are?'

'Grant Davies. I'm meant to be meeting Denver here at nine.'

'Ah, yes, Mr Davies,' she said with a nod, then reached out and grasped his outstretched hand. It was large, and had the calluses of a working man. Standing this close to him made her feel petite and feminine, and although she always endeavoured to be feminine, rarely did anyone make her feel petite.

'Grant will do,' he said.

'Denver should be here shortly, along with the electrician. Jeff I think it was. Do you know him?' Taylor asked.

Grant shook his head. 'I'm pretty new in town, actually. Denver's thrown me a bit of work, doing things for a couple of his friends who were renovating—painting and plastering, that sort of thing. He thought I'd be perfect to help you out here.'

His comment surprised her. She'd thought Denver's recommendations were people he knew well, but if he was happy with the man's work, surely she would be too.

'Knock, knock,' said another man as he walked into the shop.

'Jeff?' Taylor asked.

'That'd be me. Jeff Abbott. And you must be Taylor? I know your sister from the produce shop and you're the spitting image of her.'

She felt a blush creep onto her cheeks. She didn't get many compliments, and it was nice to hear someone say how much she looked like Alex, because everyone considered Alex beautiful.

'Yes, I'm Taylor, Alex's younger sister.'

'So you're going to open a bakery. That'll be nice. As far as I'm concerned, there isn't much that smells better than freshly baked bread. You know, if you think you might need a hand, either behind the counter or with the baking, my wife, Cathy, is a real whizz in the kitchen, and she's had some experience in retail.'

'I'll certainly keep that in mind, Jeff. Is she looking for a part-time job?'

He laughed. 'Looking, no, but it'd be nice to see her get out of the house a bit more ... and bringing in a bit of money couldn't hurt, could it?'

Just as she started to answer, Denver arrived. 'Sorry I'm late. I take it you've all met?'

'We have. So, what do we do first?' Taylor asked.

Taylor watched as Denver, with a bit of help from both Grant and Jeff, stomped around listening for weaknesses in the floorboards. He pulled up a few to check the foundations, but if Denver's body language was anything to go by, she suspected the building was in pretty good condition.

Grant's body language, on the other hand, puzzled her. She could only hope Denver knew more about what he was looking for than Grant did.

When Denver finished, he stood wiping his dusty hands on his jeans, his smile suggesting he was happy with what he'd found.

'You're in luck—this old building is as sound as I had suspected,' he said, looking at Taylor. Then, turning to Grant and Jeff, he issued instructions and said his farewells so they could get started.

Grant headed outside and began to pull the boards off the window to inspect the sill, and Jeff headed for the office to locate the fuse box, which he'd called the breaker panel.

'I'm going over to the hardware store for a few things, but I should be back in about a half-hour,' Taylor said as she walked out the door.

'We'll be fine,' Grant said, looking up from the sill and giving her a look which made her breath catch momentarily.

As she walked down the street, she took several slow breaths and by the time she walked into the hardware store she'd completely regained her composure. Twenty minutes later, she returned with a bucket, a pair of extra-heavy-duty rubber gloves, a bottle of something the woman at the service desk had guaranteed her would clean the glass, a sturdy scrub brush, four rolls of paper towels, a rubber squeegee, and a stepladder.

By eleven-thirty, she'd only made a small dent toward cleaning the front window but, with all the physical effort, she was roasting. She pulled off her light-weight hoodie and tied it around her waist, and when she looked up afterwards her gaze drifted toward Grant. He, too, must have gotten hot because he'd stripped off his shirt and now wore only a singlet. Even through the glass, she could see his muscles ripple beneath his tanned skin as he dug out the rot along the edge of the sill.

Perhaps he felt her staring, because when he looked up, he caught her eye and winked.

Embarrassed at getting sprung watching him, she shrugged and went back to cleaning the glass.

Not long afterwards, Denver arrived. 'How's it all going?' he asked no one in particular as he surveyed the progress in the front of the shop.

'Everything's good here,' Grant replied, stretching out his back as he walked in through the front door.

Again, Taylor's eyes were drawn to Grant, only this time she quickly looked away before he'd noticed.

When Jeff came in from the back area, Denver turned to him. 'What are your thoughts on the time-frame now that you've made a start, Jeff?'

'Week and a half—maybe a bit less if I'm lucky.'

Denver turned to Taylor. 'You happy with that?'

'Absolutely, but I don't think it would make a difference if I wasn't, would it?'

Denver shrugged. 'I could get someone else in to give Jeff a hand.'

Taylor shot a glance toward Jeff, now focussed on a non-existent spot on the floor. 'No, it's fine. This is all going so much faster than I'd hoped as it is.'

When she caught Jeff's eye he smiled.

Denver turned to Grant. 'By the time you finish the windows, Jeff should have made enough progress so you can get started with repairs to the walls. Then next week you can get started on the painting.'

'Sounds good,' Grant replied.

'Well, at the rate I'm going I'll be at least another day just getting this window cleaned,' Taylor said with a frown.

'What are you using?' Denver asked.

When she showed him the soap solution and the bucket and brush, he rolled his eyes and shrugged. 'No wonder it's taking you so long. You need a paint scraper. Come with me down to the hardware store, and I'll buy you some lunch at the café next door while we're out.'

She looked down at her crumpled shirt and cringed. 'Like this?'

'Trust me, they've seen worse in there,' he said, chuffing out a breath.

'Do I need to lock up?' she asked, looking over her shoulder at Grant, who'd gone back outside to continue working on the window. She figured both he and Jeff would be going out for lunch as well.

'Around here? No, don't worry about it. These guys will sort themselves out. Come on.'

CHAPTER 4

1984 – Eve

'That was the best hot and sour soup I've ever tasted,' I said as I wiped my mouth with the paper napkin. The restaurant was crowded, and I could see people waiting near the door for a table, a sure sign I wasn't the only one impressed with the food.

Andrew smiled. 'Glad you liked it. It's my favourite spot to eat whenever I'm in the city—nothing fancy, just really good food.'

We paid the bill, each taking care of our own share, and started the short trip back to the hotel. The balmy evening air was more typical of September than August, so the short-sleeved top I'd worn with my jeans proved to have been the right choice. Andrew had also dressed for the Indian summer weather, wearing a green tee-shirt that brought out the colour in his eyes, and a pair of jeans. As I glanced at him, I felt as though I was in a dream—free from the constraints of living in a small town where you couldn't go anywhere without being known. Here, Andrew and I were just two people in a city where a black man and a white woman walking together down the street would be nothing to take notice of. It was liberating to simply blend in.

As we continued along the sidewalk, we came across people coming in the other direction, and the third time this happened my bare arm rubbed up against Andrew's, sending tingles through my whole body. When I looked over at him and caught his smile, I felt certain we'd be sleeping in the same room that night.

When we arrived back at the hotel, we passed the cocktail lounge on the way to the elevator.

'Care for a nightcap?' he asked, nodding toward the crowded bar area.

I looked in, not recognising anyone but suspecting some were very likely to be from our course. Intuition made the hair on my arms prickle, telling me it would be much smarter to keep our friendship slightly more discreet.

'You know, I think I've got some Bailey's in my mini-bar. Will that do you for a nightcap?'

Again, a slow smile touched his full lips, and his green eyes grew intense as he nodded. 'Sure.'

As I opened the door of my room, my heart started racing and I could barely breathe.

I knew so little about this man, and literally nothing about his private life. And he knew nothing about mine, although I was certain he couldn't have missed the diamond ring I wore as I'd made no attempt to hide it.

He wore no jewellery, but that didn't necessarily mean he wasn't married. He had said something about leaving food out for his cats which didn't seem like something a married man would have to do.

This was all on me. I was the adulteress. I was inviting him to my room, knowing full well what would happen. And although a small part of me felt horrible for betraying Don, I was helpless against the sheer power of attraction drawing us together.

As soon as the door shut behind me, we came together like sex-starved teenagers. It had never been this way with Don. Our relationship hadn't turned sexual until we were engaged, and even then it had never been this passionate.

I was a different person—someone with no inhibitions.

I was a seductress, luring this handsome man into my den of wrongdoing.

And I loved every moment of it.

~~*~~

I woke at first light. In our hurry to get into bed the night before, we'd failed to even think about shutting the drapes. Now, pale light streamed into the room through the sheer curtains. I rolled over, and there he was, still sound asleep. This perfect specimen of a man, his caramel-coloured skin flawless against the heavy white hotel sheets, lay only inches from my side.

I luxuriated in the ability to watch him breathing—feeling no remorse, no guilt and, amazingly no shame in my nakedness. I figured this must be what they talk about when describing an out-of-body experience because I, Evelyn Gold, now Evelyn Harrison, of boring old Masons Flat, California, couldn't be the woman in this bed with a near stranger.

A pleasant soreness between my legs reminded me of the night before. I'd never experienced anything like that—neither of us able to get enough of the other—until we finally dropped off to sleep in exhaustion. How many times had he become aroused, each time as intense as the previous? Was it three? Or could it have been four times?

I reached up, touching my bruised lips, then ran my tongue over them, remembering how it had felt having his mouth caressing mine.

Perhaps I'd moved, because he stirred and his eyes opened slowly.

'Good morning, gorgeous,' he said, his voice deep and filled with happiness.

'Good morning, yourself.' I replied, surprised at how natural this felt.

'What's the time?'

I rolled over and looked at the clock radio by the bed, then turned back to him and smiled. 'Six-thirty. The first session isn't until eight-thirty so we've got plenty of time.'

A wicked smile touched his lips as he reached up and stroked the side of my face, letting his hand trail slowly down my neck, across the top of my shoulder, and finally sliding down my waist until it found the small of my back. Then he gently pulled me toward him until our bodies were touching once again.

'Plenty of time for what, my little vixen?' he asked with a quirked eyebrow.

When our mouths met, every inch of me throbbed with want.

He quickly rolled onto his back, pulling me on top, and within moments I experienced the now familiar sensation as he entered me.

We made love again, this time more slowly, and in the light of day.

And once again, I had no regrets.

What had I become?

~~*~~

The last presentation finished at three-thirty.

'We have to stay in touch, don't you agree? I mean, we can't let this be a one-off encounter.' The now familiar timber of his voice sent tingles through me, as did the realisation that what had taken place between us meant as much to him as it did to me.

We'd both packed up our belongings but neither of us had made a move to leave the conference room. We'd checked out after breakfast, so there was nowhere private we could go or I'm sure I would have suggested it.

I smiled, swallowing through the longing building in my throat. I'd known Andrew for only a little more than thirty hours and yet the thought of never seeing him again gave me a greater sense of loss than I'd ever experienced. I brushed away my feelings, trying to speak normally. 'Of course. Although ...'

'Yes, I know. I saw the ring. You don't have to say anything.'

'Perhaps it would be best if we put this down as a lapse of judgement, you know? Consider it one of those one-night stands people talk about?'

He sighed with a heaviness that matched my own pain as he leaned in close. 'This was not a one-night stand, Eve. I think you know that.'

I smiled, glad I hadn't read more into it than I should have. I had nothing to compare this to, but deep in my heart I knew we were meant to be together—that what had happened last night couldn't be a one-off incident.

But what about Don—my husband—the man I'd promised to be faithful to? I really did love him. My feelings for Andrew didn't erase my feelings for Don. It was just the feelings I had for Andrew were different. One side of me thought they might be more spiritual. The other side of me suspected I was being ridiculous. We barely knew each other.

I swallowed again, trying to think this through. 'You won't be able to call me. I mean, no one can ever know. I live in a small town, where word travels quickly. This must be our secret.'

'Of course. I'll wait to hear from you. That's fine.'

He started to hand me a business card, but I shook my head. 'I can't have that on me—and I've nowhere to hide it.'

He gave me a knowing nod, then pulled out a sheet from his notebook and, in the most deliciously elegant handwriting, wrote out a phone number and put the name Sylvia next to it. 'Here. Please, take this. Call me if you think there is somewhere we can meet. I'll come, any time, day or night. You say when and where and I promise I'll be there.'

We didn't dare kiss—people were everywhere—but he walked me to my car and stood watching until I'd pulled out of the parking garage. I gazed at him in my rear-view mirror, every inch of me wanting to turn around, get out and run to him for one last embrace, one last kiss. Instead, I sniffed back my tears and drove off.

As I crossed the Bay Bridge heading for home, panic set in. I'd never worried about birth control with Don because we'd been trying, unsuccessfully, to conceive. What if our difficulty wasn't because of me? What if I was extremely fertile? And what if Andrew was as well? What if one of the condoms he'd used wasn't effective? How often did they fail? My hands became clammy, and I could literally feel the blood rushing to my vital organs. I turned on the radio, rolled down the window, and tried to breathe in deeply to calm myself.

Fate couldn't be so cruel as to give me a child who would obviously not be my husband's, could it? No, I couldn't let those thoughts haunt me. I mean, seriously, what were the odds?

The two-hour drive gave me plenty of time to think, to reflect on what I'd done, the risks I'd taken, and the deceit I'd engaged in. Logically, I knew I'd done a horrible thing. Yet emotionally, I still held no remorse. I was glad I'd met Andrew, and that we'd spent the night together. Glad that, with his help, I had discovered marvellous things about not only his body, but also about my own.

And that made me even more afraid of what lay ahead—knowing my punishment for betraying my marriage vows with another man would be a physical longing which might never again be satisfied for the rest of my life.

CHAPTER 5

Present Day

Taylor followed as Denver headed straight to the aisles with all the painting accessories. He selected two scrapers—one made of plastic and a smaller one with a razor blade in it.

'Try to use this one for the most part,' he said, holding up the larger one, 'but for stubborn spots, use this one.'

As he handed her the tools, his fingers brushed her hand. She looked up at him, arching a brow, surprised by the surge his touch sent through her.

'This little one will leave deep scratches in the glass if you aren't careful, so make sure you have it flat against the glass, not on an angle,' he said, seemingly oblivious to what she'd felt.

'Right—got it,' Taylor replied, tearing her eyes away from his face to focus on the scrapers.

'Need anything else while we're in here?' Denver asked, his tone professional, helpful. He owned the hardware store with his brother and, at this moment, seemed to have taken on the persona of proprietor without even realising it.

'Oh, I should probably give you a key to the shop—so you can come and go as necessary, don't you think?'

'Yeah, that'd be great—I was thinking of asking for one.'

After they'd organised two spare keys, they made their way to the café.

Taylor was impressed by the clean café. In addition to offering all kinds of sandwiches, the glass display held several salads to choose from, along with quiches and frittatas that could be heated up. They also had a small selection of desserts.

Even so, the most prevalent aroma in the shop was fresh lavender, making Taylor wonder where they got their bread and desserts.

'I'll have a plate with a bit of each of the salads, thanks,' she said to the girl behind the glass display cabinet. 'They look delicious—do you make them?'

The young girl shook her head. 'Mom does all the salads in the morning, as soon as she gets back with the bread.'

'Oh, so you don't bake on the premises?' Taylor asked, knowing full well the answer would be no.

The young girl shook her head again. 'Mom drives over to Sonora to get it and then comes back to do the salads. I don't come in until we open at eight and I stick around to help with the lunch crowd.'

Taylor looked around the shop. There was just one other couple; hardly what she'd have called a crowd, but it hadn't yet gone twelve. Maybe most people came in after twelve. Or maybe she was a fool to think this town needed a bakery. For the first time since the idea had struck her, she wondered if she had set herself up to be a massive failure. Maybe it hadn't only been the renovation costs keeping anyone from leasing the old butcher shop.

Once Denver had his sandwich and a hefty serving of the pasta salad on his plate, they made their way to a table near the window. While Denver scoffed down his lunch, Taylor sat facing the street, watching the few pedestrians who passed by.

Disappointment skirted around the edges of her mind, until a line from an old movie pushed it away. *Build it, and they will come.* She couldn't give up before she even got started.

She glanced back to the counter at the young girl, deciding there and then that she'd come in early tomorrow and talk to the girl's mother. She would then pay a visit to the principals at the two schools, and she'd drop in to see Darleen about making savoury items to sell at the bar. Afterwards, she'd call in at the hotel. She'd have plenty of customers, and the bakery would be fine. It might not be an instant success, but she'd never shied away from hard work before and shouldn't start doing so now.

Denver's voice took her by surprise. 'You look lost in thought. Or isn't the food any good?'

'Sorry, no, the salads are lovely. I ... I was just noticing how quiet it is in the town. I mean, it's lunchtime but I wouldn't exactly call this place crowded.'

Denver surveyed the room, then gave her a crooked smile. 'Welcome to Masons Flat. We're a small town with loyal customers, but not a lot of them. Are you worried about the bakery?'

'A little, but you're right about loyalty. I'll be fine. I'll win over the locals and then branch out if I need more customers.'

Denver cocked his head. 'That a girl—you'll be fine. So, when do you want to go look at ovens?'

'Probably Monday.'

'Monday ... okay, I'll see what I can do about getting the day off.'

'Oh, you don't need to come with me. I mean, I'd love your company, but I know how busy you are. Besides, I'll take the opportunity to have lunch with Casey while I'm in Sacramento. Can I ring you, though, if I have concerns?'

'Absolutely. I always have my cell phone in my pocket. If they give you any trouble, don't hesitate to call.'

~~*~~

Taylor couldn't believe how sore her arms and shoulders were by the end of the afternoon, but she was pleased with the result. She'd managed to remove all the paint from the glass, which now sparkled. She stretched, throwing her shoulders back, taking the opportunity to glance over toward Grant. He'd finished digging out the rot on the large east-facing window and was putting plastic wood into the cavities. She was grateful he'd stayed away from the one she was working on, because she wasn't sure she could have concentrated on her own tasks if he'd been right there next to her.

She made her way to the sink at the back of the shop, dumped the water and rinsed out the brush, then ducked her head into the office to see how Jeff was getting on.

'Everything's fine—I haven't come across anything unexpected, so the estimate I gave Denver this morning is about right. I should be done by the end of next week, if not earlier.'

'Perfect,' she replied, thinking about what he'd said about his wife. 'Do you want to ask your wife if she could come in one day and talk to me about some work? The more I think about it, it would be nice to have some help.'

'Seriously? Yeah, of course I will. I'll talk to her tonight and let you know what she thinks. Should I get her to type up a resume, too?'

'That sounds like a plan. It'll give me all her contact details and everything. Are you about ready to call it a day?'

'Twenty minutes, if that's okay with you.'

'Fine,' she said, then left him to finish.

She made her way outside to where Grant was finishing up, stopping a few feet from him. She waited quietly as he finished, admiring the perfection he seemed to be striving for.

He must have felt her presence because he eventually looked up. When their eyes met, she again had the sensation of all the oxygen being sucked out of her lungs. It unsettled her, yet at the same time, was not unpleasant. 'And are you about ready to call it a day?' she asked.

He stood, wiped his hands on his jeans, and nodded. 'Yeah, I think so. I'll get started on that front window tomorrow, and then on the smaller ones at the back. I didn't want to get in your way today.'

'That sounds good. Jeff hopes to be done in the office tomorrow, so I'll have a good look at it and decide what colour I want it. After you finish with the windows, you can get started on the walls in there.' She smiled, hoping to soften what she feared may have sounded like barked instructions—especially since Denver was actually their boss, not her.

'Sure thing. So, we'll meet here tomorrow, at what, about seven-thirty?'

She should have realised tradesmen liked to get an early start. 'Perfect,' she replied, albeit a touch reluctantly. For a moment she considered giving him the extra key she'd had cut, but something made her stop short of saying it. It was nice being in control of who worked and when.

~~*~~

When Taylor pulled up in front of the bakery at twenty past seven the next morning, Grant and Jeff were already there, standing on the corner having a chat.

'Sorry, am I late?' she said as she got out of her car.

They both said good morning, then Grant quirked an eyebrow. 'Years of being early to work—always helps make a good impression with the boss, you know?'

She let them in and then proceeded to have a good look around the space. Now that the boards had been removed from the window facing Mason Street, the space looked much larger.

'Why do you think they'd boarded up the window? I'd half expected the glass to be damaged, but it looks fine to me.'

'You know,' Jeff said, answering her, 'I think they originally did it to keep it from getting vandalised, and then it just stayed like that. The shop's been empty for quite a while ... at least three or four years anyway, maybe longer. The last guy who ran the butcher shop tried to sell the business but, when he didn't get any takers, gave up and moved to Florida. The owners of the property weren't locals and must not have been too worried about the shop because the agent never really did much in the way of advertising. And then it turned out the agent was a bit of a crook.'

Taylor nodded as he spoke, recalling Alex telling her about the crooked agent who'd tried to secure a number of the properties for a developer—something about them trying to turn the town into a western-themed tourist attraction. A frown tightened her brow at the thought. If he'd been successful, this opportunity would never have arisen. She would no doubt still be in Melbourne and quite possibly helping build up someone else's bakery business. It was funny how things worked out sometimes—the old silver lining theory.

She turned toward the door when she heard footsteps.

'Good morning everyone,' Denver said as he walked in.

Grant and Jeff said hello, and then they discussed the plan for the day's work. When Jeff went to the back and Grant went outside to get started, Taylor stayed in the front of the shop with Denver.

'So, what are your plans for today?' he asked.

'I think I'll go up the street to the café and see if I can talk to the owner about supplying bread rolls and desserts to them. After that, I want to drop across the road to see Alex. I might even see if they can squeeze me in at the beauty salon. I've got a hot date tomorrow night, so I wouldn't mind getting a manicure and a trim,' she said, tilting her head and running her hand through her long locks in a way she hoped looked provocative.

'A hot date, eh? Should I be jealous?'

She shook her head as she puffed out a breath. 'Seeing as how I don't know what time I might finish at the beauty salon, are you able to check in on these guys in the afternoon and lock up if I'm not back in time?'

He nodded vigorously. 'Of course—I intend to do that every afternoon.'

'You're a champion, Denver. I am so looking forward to a cup of coffee. I dashed out to meet these guys and haven't even had my first cup yet.'

'You know, I should be the one to let these guys in each morning, too—that way I can make sure they have enough planned to keep busy.'

The thought of having a sleep-in was tempting. She'd had years of four a.m. starts, and once the bakery opened, she'd be right back to them. It was a pleasant change not to have to be up before dawn.

'Would you mind? I'll probably still call in most days, to see what I can do with respect to cleaning or whatever, but having a couple of weeks of sleeping-in does sound rather nice.'

When Denver laughed, it occurred to her he was no doubt up by dawn most mornings himself. 'Of course I don't mind.'

She smiled, again grateful for his help. 'Okay then ... I guess I'll see you tomorrow night? At about six-thirty?'

'You will indeed,' Denver said, tipping his hat in farewell as he headed outside and down the street toward his truck.

When Denver drove off, she ducked out to the back of the shop and said goodbye to Jeff and then stopped outside to say goodbye to Grant, who was still working on the front window. She marvelled at his strong hands as he chiselled out a small amount of rot at the bottom of the glass.

'This window doesn't look as bad as the other,' she said when he turned and caught her eye.

'No, it's had the protection of the awning, so it's in pretty good shape. I think the little ones outside the office and back area might be a different story but, with a bit of luck, I should have them all done today.'

'Oh, I wasn't trying to hurry you. So ... if I don't see you this afternoon, have a nice weekend.'

His eyes narrowed for a fraction of a second before his face broke out in a broad smile—one that didn't quite reach his eyes. 'You too,' he replied, chewing on his bottom lip.

She started to head to her car, but decided not to move it, so she spun on her heel and headed down the street in the opposite direction. As she did so, she glanced over toward Grant. He was still watching her intently. A shiver ran down her spine, taking her by surprise. It wasn't the same as the sensation she'd had watching his rippling muscles and strong hands. This sensation was different, and it made her feel uneasy.

Not knowing what to make of it, she picked up her pace as she headed to the café.

CHAPTER 6

1984 – Eve

'How was the conference, honey?' Don asked from the sofa where he'd clearly been watching a basketball game. He had a beer in one hand, and there were three empties on the coffee table.

I looked at him through eyes that would never see him quite the same way ever again. He was a handsome man—many of my friends had expressed their envy about how lucky I'd been to snag such a handsome husband—that certainly wasn't the issue. I couldn't quite put words to it, but it was as though he had no intensity about him. Perhaps my eyes had been opened to something that Don didn't have, something I'd never missed because I hadn't even known it existed.

Until now.

'It was okay. Pretty dry material, but it gave me lots of credit so I'm glad I went.'

He drained the last of the beer and set the empty can down with the others. 'That's good. I still don't think there's any real need for you to keep up your certification, but if it makes you happy, so be it.'

'It makes me happy,' I replied, wondering if another conference might be the easiest way to see Andrew again.

'I had a steak and a couple of eggs a few hours ago, so there's no need for you to cook unless you want something? Did you have dinner before you left the city?' he asked, looking at me with his head cocked.

I knew the look. He was hoping I would say I had already eaten, and we could go to bed early.

But the last thing I wanted right now was to go to bed with him. I hated myself momentarily—hated that I had changed and would never again enjoy our basic style of lovemaking. I hated, too, that if I dared to suggest anything different, he would know I'd learned more than accounting standards at the conference.

'No, I didn't. Think I'll have a couple of eggs myself,' I replied. Then, thinking what would take the longest to prepare, I added, 'soft-boiled ... on toast.'

I headed into the kitchen and let him go back to his basketball game, and when we finally made our way up to bed a good while later, I said I was exhausted from the drive. He kissed my forehead, rolled over, and immediately began snoring. For once, I was grateful he'd had so many beers.

Over the next few days, I avoided sex with Don by fixing elaborate dinners that took extra preparation time so that it was quite late by the time I washed up.

And then, after Don dropped off to sleep and I heard the rhythm of his deep breathing, I allowed myself the luxury of thinking about Andrew—and about what we'd done. And just thinking about him made my body respond with desire for something I couldn't have.

~~*~~

I pulled up in front of a tired-looking motel off Highway Five a few minutes after seven, exactly six days since Andrew and I had parted.

I had gotten the idea to visit a friend I'd met in college. She lived in Los Banos, where she'd taken a job with a smaller accounting firm, but had stopped working when she had a baby. We'd kept in touch, and she'd been pestering me to come for a visit for a while now—telling me she was bored out of her brain. When it occurred to me I might be able to meet Andrew somewhere near her place, I rang and arranged to come over Saturday afternoon. Don had been thrilled. He thought it was good for me to spend some time with this woman and her baby. I'm certain he hoped it would trigger some maternal instincts in me because we were, technically, still trying to conceive. Once the visit had been arranged and Don was happy for me to stay the night, I'd rung Andrew from a payphone. He was ecstatic with the plan and instantly agreed to book a motel on the outskirts of town under the name of Johnson.

I tapped on the door—room 212, upstairs—and he immediately opened it.

If I'd had any doubt about meeting him again, it was quashed the moment our eyes met. Days had gone by, but it might as well have been hours. The connection remained, perhaps even stronger than it had been.

He pulled me into his arms for the kiss I'd been craving since we'd parted and then gently removed my clothing and led me over to the large, if not exactly luxurious, bed.

We made love as we had done the night at the conference, and every inch of my body remembered him and responded to him in ways I would never have imagined before meeting him.

With our passion finally satiated, he rolled onto his side and ran a finger down the side of my face. 'I've missed you,' he said in the familiar honey-smooth tones that stirred me once again.

'And I've missed you, too. It's been so hard, pretending everything at home is normal.'

'You could leave him, you know. You could move to Santa Cruz with me, and we could live in sin and swim in the ocean and make love on the beach every night.'

I laughed, thinking how wonderful his fantasy sounded while at the same time knowing the woman in that image was someone else, not me. I was a housewife and bookkeeper from a small country town. I'd never, in a million years, have thought I'd become someone's mistress, and certainly couldn't see myself taking the next step of living in sin, as he'd called it, in a beach community.

'If only I could,' I said, grabbing his hand and interlocking my fingers with his. I pulled my arm up between us and held his hand close to my heart.

'Tell me something about yourself, Andrew. I mean, I know so little about you.'

'You know me ... in here,' he said, tapping our intertwined hands against my chest.

'I'm serious. Tell me about your life.'

A lazy smile crossed his lips as he considered his words. 'I live in a condominium not far from the beach, with two cats. I work in Cupertino, but I don't mind the commute—it's worth it to live near the beach. I surf most mornings, unless I have a really early meeting that I have to get to. I tried the large accounting firms, but it wasn't for me. Now I'm the Financial Controller for a company that imports components for computers. It's quite a low-stress job for the salary, but best of all it leaves me plenty of time to surf and swim.'

'What about your family? Are they in California too?'

'I have one sister who lives in San Diego, and a brother who still lives in Chicago. I was born in Chicago, but came out to California on a scholarship to UC Santa Barbara. I fell in love with the Pacific Ocean, as did my sister when she came out to visit me a few times.'

'And your parents? One of them must be African American?'

When he smiled, his green eyes glistened. 'Yes, my father was African-American, but my mother was as pale as a china doll. She was French—an illegitimate descendant of Napoleon, or so she liked to claim. I got his skin colouring and her eyes,' he said, raising a brow provocatively as he flashed a smile.

'You said, was, not are—so I take it your parents are no longer living?'

'My dad died of cancer, and my mother took to the bottle shortly afterwards. Within a few years, she died too. I don't think she could face living without him. They were a match made in Heaven. She was lost without him.'

My heart ached for her—for this woman who had borne the man who quite clearly was intended to be my match made in Heaven. I knew how she felt. I could no longer imagine life without Andrew any more than I could imagine life without air. I swallowed back my emotions and sighed.

'What about you? Tell me something about who you are,' he said, his tone still smooth but more serious now.

'Me?' What could I tell him? There was nothing terribly interesting about my life.

'Yes. I want to know who Eve is—where she comes from, what's made her the person she is.'

He propped himself up on his free arm, but allowed me to keep our intertwined hands close to my chest.

'Well, it's all pretty boring, actually. I was born in a small town, went through school in that same small town, and still live in that same small town now.' Once again, I refrained from mentioning the name of the town. I couldn't risk him driving up out of curiosity, as much as I'd get a thrill from it. 'When I got good grades in high school, my father agreed I should go to college, so off I went to San Francisco State University. No one was more surprised than me when I was offered a job in the audit division of a large and rather prestigious accounting firm. I had to take the job—it was such an opportunity, you know?'

He nodded. 'Yes, I do know. I was the same. It wasn't my heart's desire, but I couldn't turn down the opportunity. Go on ... then what?'

I drew in a deep breath, remembering how I'd given in to the pressure from Don, and how my father had backed him up. 'D—' I stopped short of saying his name, again concerned Andrew might try to find me, and started again. 'My husband also grew up in our town. He was friends with my brother, a few years ahead of me in school, and he had always teased me about us getting married one day. When he learned that I was going off to college, he gave me his school ring and told me to stay true to him. He bought the butcher shop business and stayed there. I came home every summer, and over Christmas and sometimes on the weekends, and we always saw each other then. He wasn't impressed when I took the job with the accounting firm, but I think he was afraid of my father so he didn't protest too much. But he did replace his school ring with a diamond one.'

I lifted my hand to show him the ring.

Andrew looked at my hand momentarily, and then focused his gaze on my eyes again. 'And then what?'

'Well, after I got my CPA, the firm started making noises about opportunities that would be coming up. They were building up their Los Angeles office and wanted more senior women there. That was the breaking point for both my husband and my father. They joined forces and convinced me it wasn't the life I wanted. A date was set for our wedding, with my father's blessing, and the rest is history.'

Andrew licked his lips and leaned forward to plant a gentle kiss on my forehead. When he pulled back, he smiled. 'You know what I think? I think everything up to now has happened as it was meant to. Otherwise, we mightn't have met, and that would have been a real tragedy.'

I took a deep breath, letting his words sink in. He was right. Everything that happened is what brought us together. When I smiled, he pulled me back on top of him and we made love once again, slowly, with tenderness, until we were both in a state of euphoria.

When I woke it was daylight and I was alone in the bed. For a fraction of a moment, I'd forgotten where I was. Then the door handle turned, and Andrew came in carrying a bag of donuts and two cups of coffee.

'Breakfast in bed,' he said. And once again, his honey-smooth voice sent tingles through my body.

I sat up, pulling the sheet up to cover myself, and then laughed as I realised there wasn't an inch of my body he wasn't already intimately familiar with.

He rolled his eyes and gave me a suggestive smile.

'Hope you like glazed. I'm not a fan of those cream-filled or chocolate-covered ones.'

I licked my lips in anticipation. 'Me neither. Simple glazed has always been my favourite.'

He watched me licking my lips and shook his head. 'How am I meant to concentrate on coffee and donuts with you doing that?'

'Sorry,' I said. But I wasn't. Not one bit. I'd never experienced this sort of sexual chemistry and teasing him about it was addictive.

We sat on the edge of the bed, eating two donuts each and drinking our coffee. When we were finished, I looked at him and sighed. 'Well, I guess I better have a shower and start thinking about going home. What time do we have to check out?'

'Eleven. Do you have to go straight back? I mean, is your husband expecting you at a certain time or do you think we could spend a bit more time together? I saw a craft market while I was out getting breakfast. We could go over and have a wander through?'

'I'd like that.'

Two hours later we'd wandered up and down every aisle of the small outdoor market. I'd bought a few trinkets—a beaded fabric horse, a small wooden car painted with red racing stripes, and a tiny stuffed cat with emerald green eyes.

'What do you want with those things? Andrew asked, not quite frowning but looking somewhat perplexed.

'I don't know. I just hated seeing them there, unloved and unwanted. I'll put them somewhere safe, to remind me of this day. The cat's eyes remind me of you, by the way.'

He threw his head back with a soft laugh.

We continued to walk in silence. We weren't holding hands, but we occasionally bumped up against each other and each time that familiar sensation coursed through my blood—the tingle telling me we were meant to be together.

When the market began to pack up, we slowly made our way back to our cars. I said goodbye with a heavy heart, yet I smiled because this time I knew our goodbye was only temporary and that we would, definitely, see each other again.

CHAPTER 7

Present Day

When Denver led her into the crowded Sonora restaurant on Saturday night, Taylor had been surprised to see how many people were waiting in both the foyer and the bar area, but by the time she'd taken her first bite of steak she'd worked out why—the food was excellent.

Patting her tummy as she finished her last bite, she set her knife and fork down and smiled at Denver. 'I haven't had such a good steak since I scored a King Island Eye Fillet at a friend's wedding, and that was only because her parents are filthy rich. And as for the baked potato, the ones here in California are so much fluffier than the ones we have at home.'

Denver hid his smile behind his napkin as he wiped his mouth, but she could see it in his eyes. She knew some men loved a woman with a good appetite. She hoped he was one of them.

'Home,' she continued, '... well, actually, I suppose this is home now, isn't it? I should say back in Melbourne.'

He placed his napkin next to his plate, rested his elbows on the edge of the table and leaned toward her. 'Can't say I know all that much about potatoes, but I'm glad you enjoyed your dinner. Can't go wrong with a steak and a baked potato, if you ask me. So, are we ready to make a move?'

When the bill arrived, Denver wouldn't allow her to pay for her share of the dinner.

'My shout next time then,' she said, not wanting to make a big deal about it.

The drive to the bar only took a few minutes and, when they walked in, Taylor was immediately reminded of the saloon in Masons Flat. From its huge bar, jukebox and small dance floor, to the tinkling sounds of glassware and the laughter of patrons sharing sociable drinks, if she hadn't seen it from the outside, she'd be forgiven for thinking she'd somehow ventured into the Gold Nugget.

'This doesn't look like a nightclub ... is it a private party?'

Denver grinned. 'Not exactly, but they don't usually have a live band here. It's the same band I hired for my thirtieth last year; Tommy and the Tripods. They sent me a message saying they were going to be here trying out some new music, so I had to come. Their music is amazing to dance to.'

They headed to a corner of the room where they had a good view of the dance floor. It was standing room only, suggesting word had gotten out about the band. It was also a slightly different clientele to those leaning up at the bar, as this group appeared to be dressed to dance.

Within a few moments the band came on, and Taylor's eyes were drawn to the few couples who hit the dance floor and started swirling and dipping like experts.

'Oh, aren't they good,' she said, leaning in to speak directly into Denver's ear.

'Wait until we get up there ... we'll put them to shame,' he replied, reaching across and taking her hand.

She laughed. 'Uh, hardly. I've never been a good dancer, and I'm not sure I want to embarrass myself just yet. Maybe if I've had a few more drinks,' she said with a laugh as she pulled her hand free and ran it through her hair. 'Me, dancing like that ... I wish.'

'You'll be fine. You simply hang on and follow my lead,' Denver said, again taking her hand and encouraging her to follow him.

She was glad of the darkness when she felt the colour draining from her face. Struggling to find her voice, she leaned forward and spoke into his ear. 'You've seriously got to be kidding. I remember saying I'd like to learn, but ...'

'The only way to learn is to just get up and do it, right? Come on, it's easy. Trust me.'

Against her better judgement, she allowed Denver to drag her onto the floor. He took both her hands and gently led her through a few basic steps but it was no use—her feet refused to go where she wanted them to.

Leaning in close to his chest, she tried again. 'Maybe I should watch for a little while first? Maybe my brain will get the idea if I watch you.

There are plenty of women here who look as though they'd be happy to oblige if you asked them to dance.'

'Really? You want me to dance with someone else?' He feigned a look of rejection, but she could see the twinkle in his eye.

She shrugged. 'For a little while. After I've watched for a bit, I promise I'll have another go.'

'If you insist,' he said as he led her off the floor and back to the corner where they'd been standing. He squeezed her hand as he gave her a kiss on the cheek. 'Don't go wandering off on me, will you?'

'Of course not,' she laughed, relieved to be left as a spectator.

Denver approached a group of women on the other side of the room that, by the way they embraced him with hugs, all seemed to know him. Finally, he led a woman with long dark hair onto the floor and they came together for a moment as he whispered something in her ear. When they began to dance, the others on the floor acted as though they were in the presence of royalty, pushing to the sides to make room for the pair. After a moment, it became clear why they'd moved aside—Denver and this woman danced as though they done it a million times before.

'They look good together, don't they,' said a male voice from beside her.

She turned, startled. 'Grant? What are you doing here?' She hadn't expected to know anyone, let alone her own tradesman.

'Denver mentioned it. He knows I'm new around here, so he said he'd introduce me to a few people if I came along tonight.'

'Oh, I see,' she said with a nod. Denver hadn't said anything to her about Grant possibly joining them.

Thankfully the loud music discouraged much conversation. She turned back to watch Denver and his partner, trying to ignore the unsettling sensation creeping over her and trying to pretend her thumping heartbeat had more to do with the spectacle of the dancers than Grant's presence. She took a few settling breaths and tried harder to focus on the dancers. When the song ended, Denver returned with the dark-haired woman in tow.

'Taylor, this is Cherise. She and I went to school together—we've known each other for ages. Cherise, Taylor is our newest resident. She's fixing up the old butcher shop and turning it into a bakery.'

Cherise smiled, exposing perfect white teeth behind luscious red lips. She was a stunner, and Taylor couldn't help but wonder just how well she and Denver knew each other.

'A bakery? How wonderful is that.' She practically purred in a voice as evocative as her appearance.

'Oh, and this is Grant Davies. Grant's been doing some work for me around town. He's a carpenter come handy-man come jack-of-all-trades. He's new in town so I figured I could introduce him to you and a few of the others.'

Grant grinned. 'Pretty much sums me up,' he said, focusing on Cherise.

'Ready to give it a go?' Denver asked, turning back to Taylor as the next song started.

She wasn't—not really—but she would have to bite the bullet sooner or later. Taking Denver's outstretched hand, she followed him onto the floor.

Her worst fears materialised. She still couldn't get her feet to do as her mind instructed, and although he displayed extreme patience, she could tell Denver was not enjoying the experience either. At her encouragement, they left the dance floor before the song ended and made their way back to the same corner.

That's when she realised Grant and Cherise were no longer there. She turned, scanning the dancers until she spotted them. They, too, looked good together—although Taylor wondered if it was simply that Cherise was such an extraordinarily beautiful woman and exquisite dancer that she would make any man look good out there.

'Can I get you a drink?' Denver asked, pulling out his wallet and dragging her attention back to him.

'I would love a glass of soda water, thanks,' she answered.

As Denver headed to the bar, she turned back to watch the dancers again. She quickly spotted Grant and Cherise as, once again, some of the dancers had cleared the floor to make room for the dark-haired beauty to show off her expertise. She moved like a ballerina, graceful and fluid as she swirled and dipped. Grant seemed to do little more than swing her around occasionally and provide a strong arm for her to cling to when the dance called for it. Cherise was clearly the one in control.

Watching them was mesmerising, and Taylor couldn't tear her eyes from them even though she felt sick with jealousy.

Jealousy.

The word nearly bowled her over.

Was she jealous of Cherise dancing with Grant?

It hadn't worried her in the slightest when she was dancing with Denver. She'd been fascinated, but she definitely hadn't felt jealous.

She angled herself to watch for Denver to return, purposely not wanting to look at the dance floor any longer.

'Here you go,' he said, handing her the glass when he finally returned.

She took it with a smile. 'Thank you. I should have gotten the drinks, seeing as how you got dinner.'

The corners of Denver's lips pulled up and his eyes twinkled. 'Don't think you're getting off the hook that easy. When you take me out—I believe you said it was your shout next time?—you can pay.'

She held up her glass and touched it to his beer glass. 'Cheers,' she said with a smile, then took a sip.

At first, Taylor successfully kept her back to the dance floor by facing Denver and trying to make casual conversation, but the loud music made it difficult to talk, so after a time she gave up and turned to watch the dancers as well. The band continued to play for another twenty minutes or so before announcing they were taking a break. Just after that, Grant and Cherise walked up.

'Great band, Denver, thanks for telling me about this place,' said Grant, stopping beside Denver.

'Yes, they remind me of the band that played at your birthday,' Cherise said as she dabbed at her forehead with a tissue.

'They are the same band. I thought I mentioned that when I texted you about coming here,' Denver said.

'Oh, maybe you did and I'd forgotten. Can I get anyone a drink?' Cherise asked, looking at their now empty glasses.

'I'd have another light beer, since you're offering,' Denver answered, then turned to Taylor. 'Did you want another soda water?'

'Sure. I'll come with you to help you carry them if you like,' Taylor offered.

'Thanks,' Cherise said, spinning on her heel and walking toward the bar.

Taylor followed, leaving Grant to talk to Denver. She couldn't help feeling a bit annoyed that Denver had invited them tonight, although with Grant new in town and Cherise apparently unattached, perhaps Denver was trying to do a bit of matchmaking. That shouldn't bother her, given she was on a date with Denver, and yet it did, and she wasn't certain how to handle her feelings.

Cherise leaned onto the bar and within moments a bartender arrived asking what he could get her. Taylor had never been served so quickly.

Anywhere.

Ever.

After ordering the drinks, Cherise turned back to her.

'So, you and Denver went to school together, right?' Taylor asked.

'Is that what he told you?' Cherise said, raising a brow as her mouth twisted into a half-smile.

'I'm pretty sure that's what he said. Didn't you?'

'Sure, we went to school together. And we dated ... until he went off to Sacramento to go to college. That's when I started dating a good friend of his, and we eventually got married. I love my husband with every fibre of my being, but I've always had a soft spot for Denver.'

Taylor blinked hard. Cherise was married? She looked for her left hand but couldn't quite see it well enough to tell if she wore a wedding ring. Then the bartender arrived and Cherise pulled out her wallet to pay for the drinks. Sure enough, there it was—a gold band on her ring finger. She wondered if Grant knew this about Cherise.

'Can you take these two?' Cherise asked, breaking into Taylor's thoughts.

Taylor looked up and spotted her soda water and a glass of beer next to it. Taking the drinks, they made their way back to where Denver and Grant were still talking.

After a few minutes, Cherise excused herself to go back to the group of girls on the other side of the room, and Grant left to find the bathrooms.

'Did you say you went to school with Cherise as well as the others in that group?'

'Yeah, we were all in the same year. Cherise and I dated for a while. She ended up marrying my best friend. Oh, don't get me wrong, we were over by then. And as for the others, we all hung out at school and danced at every opportunity. Cherise and I even competed a few times ... one of our teachers was really into the whole competition scene and took us down to Los Angeles. We didn't win, but it was sure fun.'

'Well, you certainly looked the real deal to me,' she answered, then took a sip of her water.

'We probably could have been the real deal, as you call it, if we'd taken it more seriously. Neither of us could be bothered to practice as much as it requires. Besides, I wanted to be a carpenter so I went off to community college to get my associate's degree and she stayed in Masons Flat. When she and Steve got married, they moved to Turlock where he has his plumbing business.'

'Turlock? Is that close?' Taylor asked.

'About an hour from here. Cherise will most likely be staying the night with one of the others.'

'I see. So she's married, but goes out with her girlfriends to bars?'

'Yeah, Steve is not into dancing at all, so he's quite happy for her to go out with the girls. Cherise is mad about him—she'd never cheat on him, if that's why you're asking.'

Taylor shook her head vigorously. 'No, not at all ... I was just ... curious.'

Denver laughed. 'Yeah, I know where you're coming from, after watching her dance with me and then Grant. She's beautiful, isn't she? But she's crazy about Steve and he's crazy about her. They've got the perfect marriage—they trust each other completely.'

'That's ... wonderful. Truly, it is.'

'Neither of them would put up with the other cheating. That's not who they are. And that's not who I am either. If I were married, I'd be happy for my wife to go out anytime with her friends as well, because she'd know if she did cheat on me, it would be the first, last and only time.' As he said the last words, his voice dropped, and Taylor saw a look of determination in his eyes that she hadn't seen before.

'I get that,' she said, then took another sip of water.

The band came back out shortly afterwards and got ready to do another set. Grant returned just long enough to grab his drink and finish it, but then went to the group of girls on the other side of the room where he received a warm welcome.

When the music started, Denver dragged her out onto the floor once again, and this time her feet behaved a bit better than before. Laughing and trying her best to focus on the basic steps, she worked hard at directing all her attention toward Denver, but even so, every now and then her eyes would seek out Grant.

'Had enough?' Denver asked when the band took what would be their last break.

'Sure, have you?'

'Yeah, I've got an early start again in the morning. Horses and cattle don't take the weekends off, even if the tradesmen do.'

'I guess I'd never thought about that, but of course they don't,' Taylor said with a shrug.

Denver looked across the room and waved, and the group, which still included Grant, waved back.

When they got back to Taylor's house, Denver walked her to the door. She dug around in her purse for the key, wondering if she should invite him in for a drink. He'd said he wanted an early night, but even so it seemed rude not to.

Luckily, he saved her from having to make the offer. 'Well, I guess it's goodnight then—like I said I've got quite an early start tomorrow. Thanks for coming out with me, I had a lot of fun.'

'So did I, and I'm looking forward to reciprocating ... soon.'

He leaned forward and placed a hand on her cheek, and when he ran his hand under her chin to lift it slightly, she closed her eyes. His kiss was gentle, barely more than a feather-soft sensation on her lips. She leaned into the kiss, but then it was over, almost before it started.

When she realised he'd stepped back away from her, she opened her eyes and smiled.

'Well, goodnight then. Sleep tight,' he said as he turned and made his way back toward his truck.

'Goodnight, Denver, drive safely,' she replied.

The moment the door closed behind her, she felt her forehead tighten into a frown.

The kiss wasn't what she'd expected their first kiss to be, but it wasn't just its lack of intensity that had her stomach twisting with unease—it was the fact that she wondered what it would have been like if Grant had been the one to take her home. Would his goodnight kiss have been full of passion?

She liked Denver. Possibly more so than any man she'd ever known before, but were her feelings those of someone in a budding romance, or of someone who had found a lifelong friend?

Images of Grant on the dance floor with Cherise teased the corners of her mind. The image was immediately followed by an echo of Denver's words about loyalty and trust.

Maybe it was just as well Denver's kiss had been just a peck. She clearly had to sort out her feelings for Grant before things with Denver went any further, because betraying Denver's trust was the absolute last thing she'd ever want to do.

CHAPTER 8

1984 – Eve

It had been eight days since I'd seen Andrew. I'd counted them out, religiously, every morning. And every time Don had touched me, on each and every one of those days, I had become more and more aware of how desperate I was to feel Andrew's hands on my body again.

Then I came up with the idea that I could go to Modesto to discuss some outstanding accounts with one of my father's biggest buyers. And surprisingly, my father, who generally preferred to deal with the cattle buyers himself because he felt they responded better to a man's strong words than those of a woman, had agreed it was a good idea. Don hadn't had a problem with it either, because he generally agreed with everything my father wanted me to do.

When I'd hung up the phone after making the arrangements with the client, the first pangs of guilt hit me. To be honest, the guilt had far less to do with cheating on my marriage vows than it did with lying to the two men who were such important parts of my life. Even so, the guilt I felt wasn't enough to dissuade me from making the call to Andrew to see if he could meet me there.

I finished up with the supplier by quarter to twelve, and then met Andrew at the motel he'd booked, several miles south of Modesto, right off Highway 99.

As I walked into the room, the fresh scent of bath soap wafted on the gentle airstream from the air-conditioning unit above the bed, and the soft strains of classical music filled the air from the tiny clock radio beside the bed, making my entire body feel at home.

While I'm not denying my reaction to seeing him was sexual—particularly given he was lounging on the bed with the sheet draped over the lower half of his naked, muscular body—the sensations overcoming me were more than that. Warmth radiated from my heart to every nerve ending throughout my body, speeding up my heartbeat and making me nearly gasp for air.

I stripped off my clothes with record speed, tossing them onto the solitary chair next to the dressing table, and we came together as we'd done each of the previous times, making love for over an hour and then lazing on the bed to discuss what was happening in our lives.

My life hadn't changed from when I'd seen him last—with the exception of my growing difficulty to pretend everything at home was fine when my true desires lay elsewhere.

Andrew's life had also changed little, remaining as perfect as it had been when I first met him. He'd surfed every morning, continued to do his job to the complete satisfaction of his superiors, and had even signed up to do a Thai cooking course at a local restaurant. His sister, however, had been unwell off and on for the last year and had recently been given some bad news. Andrew warned me that, if she didn't respond to the experimental treatment, he might have to go to San Diego. She had two young daughters and an ex-husband who was far from the model father. She wanted Andrew, not her ex-husband, to raise the girls if anything happened to her.

Fear engulfed me. Fear that if Andrew went to San Diego, I might never see him again. I took a deep breath and tried to put it out of my mind. She was young, so surely the experimental treatment would be successful.

'I have a thought,' Andrew said, his tone still holding the serious note from when he'd mentioned his sister's illness. 'Perhaps we should get a post office box so I can write to you. I know you don't want me to contact you by phone or mail at your home, but I need to have some way to contact you. Particularly given the situation with my sister.'

'Okay,' I replied, thinking it through. 'That should be fine, so long as it's in your name. Do you get two keys when you rent one?'

'I'm sure we can arrange to have two keys. And certainly, it will all be in my name. Is Modesto a good place, or should we get somewhere closer to where you live, somewhere you could get to once or twice a month, for instance?'

I thought hard. Modesto was only an hour's drive. Close enough that, surely, I could find a reason to be gone for a few hours now and then to take a drive down, and far enough away that I would be terribly unlucky to see anyone I knew.

'Yes, I think I can make it work. Should we go there now?' I knew time wasn't on my side today, and that both my father and Don would be expecting me back soon.

We showered and dressed and headed into the middle of town to find the post office. I followed him, parking a bit down the street in front of a small gift store. Not knowing how long it might take, I headed into the store to have a poke around. The store smelled musty, but there were a few items which intrigued me—the main one being a six-inch by eight-inch metal box with a green-eyed Persian cat on the top. When I picked it up, I knew I had to have it. I'd been wondering where to store the trinkets I'd bought at the market when Andrew and I had last been together, and this box would be perfect.

With my precious purchase in hand, I headed back outside. Spotting a bakery across the street, and not seeing any sign of Andrew returning, I decided to duck in there to buy a loaf of fresh sourdough bread.

It wasn't long after I'd returned to my car that Andrew walked up. I opened the passenger door for him to sit with me.

'Here you go,' he said, handing me one of the keys.

I held the key for a moment, then picked up the box and showed it to him. 'I think I'll put the key in here, along with those trinkets I bought at the market last time we met. They've been in my glove compartment, as I wasn't sure where to put them.'

He shook his head. 'You and your green-eyed cats,' he said, giving me a broad smile.

'It'll help me get through the days until we see each other again. And I know exactly the right place to stash this box.'

He cocked his head, smirking. 'You've given that a bit of thought.'

'Yes, well you were in the post office for a long time,' I replied. 'Also, long enough for me to check out the bakery across the road. The sign says they have the best sourdough bread outside San Francisco. I've bought a loaf and if it's as good as they say, it might give me an excuse to drive down here from time to time, you know?'

'Perfect,' he said, reaching out and taking my hand. 'And if you've got time to get here to check the box, you may even have enough time to meet me here once in a while.'

We said goodbye in the car, as even though I'd have liked to get out and give him a big hug and kiss, I feared a black man and white woman embracing on the street might draw attention, and the last thing I wanted was for someone to start to pay attention and then recognise me.

~~*~~

I decided to go home first before heading into the butcher shop, but as I entered the kitchen, I stopped dead in my tracks. A bouquet of red roses sat on the table alongside a card from Don. I gulped, grateful I'd decided to drop by the house first.

I'd completely forgotten it was our anniversary.

I carried the bread back to the car so he wouldn't know I'd come home, and headed into town.

When I walked into the butcher shop, Don was busy with Mrs Miller, a fussy old woman who never made any decision in a hurry. I nodded and smiled, and he did the same before turning back to assist her. I carried the bag with the loaf of bread and my precious metal box, now full of trinkets and a special key, into my office, grateful for the few moments I'd have before Don would come in to speak to me.

I put the loaf of bread on my desk and grabbed the box, pushing my desk chair out of the way. A few months earlier, I'd noticed one of the floorboards under the desk had come loose—no doubt from me rolling my chair back and forth and stomping around in the heavy boots I often wore—and when I'd pulled at it, the board had come up revealing enough space between the floorboards and the joist underneath to place something that needed to be hidden. At the time, I'd thought of money or important papers, but right now it made the perfect place to hide the evidence of my secret rendezvous. I was grateful I'd never gotten around to mentioning it to Don.

That night, when we got back to the house after work, I pretended to be surprised by the roses and pulled out the card I'd purchased from the measly selection at the small grocery store in town. I also showed him the bread I'd purchased in Modesto, planting the seed for further trips.

We quickly showered and changed, and Don took me to Sonora to the most expensive restaurant in town, where we drank champagne and dined on steak and lobster. When we finished eating, he took my hands over the table and stared into my eyes with more passion than I'd seen in him for many months.

'Happy anniversary, darling,' he said, rubbing my hands with his thumbs in a way that used to make me tingle with love. Tonight, I struggled to keep from pulling my hands away from his.

'Happy anniversary,' I said, giving him a sweet smile, hoping to erase the sensation of being the worst traitor on the planet. How could I have made love to another man on my wedding anniversary?

'Every day for the rest of my life, I will be thankful you agreed to marry me. We're so good together, darling. The only thing that could make me happier would be having a house full of kids.'

I swallowed hard, hoping my smile hadn't faded. 'It's not as if we haven't tried,' I said under my breath, thinking about all the times I'd obliged him when he wanted to have sex.

Obliged. I'd never thought of it that way before. I used to enjoy making him happy, without even knowing there could be more to it than that. But I would never be that person again.

'Hmmm ... I can't wait to get you home so we can try a little harder,' he replied, raising a brow and running his tongue across his top lip in anticipation.

Dread washed over me at the thought. I'd successfully managed to avoid sex with Don on the previous occasions when I'd been with Andrew. Tonight, I feared, I wouldn't be so lucky.

I tried my best to look interested, and squeezed his hands slightly before gently extricating mine.

'I really must go find the ladies room, darling,' I managed to say in a soft whisper, desperately needing to get away from him for a few minutes to gather my thoughts.

By the time I returned to the table, he'd already paid the bill.

'Ready to go?' he asked, looking at me with an appetite that had nothing to do with food.

'Sure,' I replied without even sitting down.

We'd barely gotten in the house when Don took my hand and led me to our bedroom. We made love as we always did: mechanically, dispassionately and, thankfully, hastily.

CHAPTER 9

Present Day

After spending all day Sunday pondering her feelings for both Denver and Grant, as well as wondering just how "married" Cherise was, Taylor found herself no closer to understanding her feelings than when she started.

When she stopped in at the bakery on Monday before heading to Sacramento to visit the supplier, she was relieved to find Denver had come and gone already and that Grant hadn't shown. She knew Denver had told Grant to hold off coming in until the rooms were ready for plastering and painting, but she'd had an uneasy feeling he might have come in anyway.

A sound from the back of the shop told her Jeff was working in the office. She walked over and stood in the doorway until Jeff looked up at her.

'Hi Taylor,' he said, standing up and wiping his hand on the leg of his jeans. 'I'm about done in here but, since you're here, do you want to have a look and make sure there are enough outlets? There is the double one on that wall, and one over here, but are those two going to be enough for you, given all the computers and printers and other gadgets people have these days?'

Taylor walked in and stood for a moment, wondering about the placement of her desk, and decided she'd want to sit with her back to the small highlight window so she could see into the bakery workspace through the doorway.

'Is it possible to have an outlet come up through the floor so that the cords for the computer come up from under the desk—to save me tripping over them all the time?'

'Sure, it shouldn't be a problem at all,' Jeff answered, bending over and tapping the floorboards. 'This one is even a bit loose, so I suspect I can pull a few up and drag the wires across from the wall. Do you want me to have a look now?'

'That'd be great, thanks.'

Jeff went out to his truck and came back with a small toolbox. Armed with a crowbar he pulled up one of the boards. Then he was able to lever up a couple of the ones beside it. When he had pulled up several, he stopped.

'We're in luck. There's plenty of space for me to crawl in from here, so I'll do this right now,' he said, putting on a cap containing a built-in light and then climbing down through the gap in the boards.

Taylor listened while he tapped and banged, and then a few minutes later he appeared, covered in dust and holding a small metal box.

'Here you go,' he said, handing her the box. 'This was on the ground, under a clean spot on one the bearers. Looks like someone hid it there, and maybe an earthquake or something shook it onto the ground below. Anyway, for it to have been hidden under there, my guess is it might contain something valuable.' He winked and then went back under the floor taking with him a small drill and a length of heavily coated wire.

Taylor took the box, reminiscent in size and shape to an Anzac Biscuit tin, and headed to the back sink to grab a paper towel to clean it off. The layer of dust made her think it must have been hidden there for quite some time.

Once clean, a pair of bright green eyes in the face of a long-haired white cat stared back at her. She felt a chill, recalling the expression about someone walking over your grave, and when she looked at her arms, all the hair stood on end.

Focusing back on the box, she shook it gently, wondering if the sound could be money sliding back and forth inside. Had the butcher kept cash there for a rainy day, or to hide it from the tax man? That seemed entirely possible, but the box looked more like it would have been owned by a woman than a man. Maybe it had been the butcher's wife, not the butcher himself, who had hidden the box?

She pulled the top off and began to investigate the contents. Inside, she found a small fabric horse, a little wooden car painted to look like a race car, and a tiny stuffed cat with emerald green eyes. She studied each item carefully and then gently set them back into the box. Then she picked up a small key that looked like it could belong to a safe deposit box. She studied it, but there was nothing on it other than a small code number. She replaced it into the box and took a deep breath.

Finally, having saved it for last, she picked up the item that held the most interest—a letter from San Diego, postmarked 1984.

Opening the envelope carefully, she found a photo of a handsome, dark-skinned man and a handwritten note. She scanned the note and was about to read it more carefully when she heard footsteps approaching.

'Anything interesting in the box?' Jeff asked, stopping a few meters behind her.

She quickly replaced the envelope and shoved the top back on the box, and set the tin on the edge of the sink before turning to smile at Jeff. 'Not really. A few trinkets—probably things from someone's childhood. Perhaps whoever put it there kept money in it from time to time, but if so, they'd removed it before putting the box back the last time.'

'Ah, too bad. Thought maybe you'd gotten a surprise win. Anyway, I've got the wires out, but I don't have the right type of outlet with me—I'll bring one from home tomorrow. It won't take long so I'll let Denver know he can organise for Grant to come in tomorrow around mid-day so he can start doing the walls in there.'

'Great, thanks Jeff. This is all coming along quite well.'

When Jeff turned and headed back to the office, she grabbed the box, called out goodbye to him as she passed, and went to her car.

She sat there for a moment, wondering about the trinkets and the key, but what held her interest was the letter. And who best to talk to about old letters discovered in secret places? Her sister, Casey, of course—the woman who'd discovered a stash of letters hidden in the old desk at their uncle's house, and the woman whom she was having lunch with in a few short hours.

CHAPTER 10

1984 – Eve

I had to tell someone.

It wasn't like I felt guilty and had to confess my sins or anything. I wasn't even certain whether I believed in God, yet somehow, I knew he or she wouldn't judge me harshly on this matter. The connection I felt with Andrew couldn't be anything other than ordained.

It was simply that I needed to speak to someone about the contradictory feelings buried deep in my heart. I loved Andrew more than I thought possible, but I also loved my husband. Was it possible to love two men simultaneously, but in different ways?

I knew if I put a voice to my feelings and talked them through with someone who had no vested interest in the outcome, it would help me to see the future more clearly. But who could I tell?

I wracked my brain for two days, trying to figure out who I could trust. For the first time in my life, I wished I had a sister. There was no way I could say anything about this to my brother. Mark loved me, and backed me up in most situations, but I knew this would probably make him angry and he would no doubt take sides with his friend. Even worse, he could mention it to our parents, and they definitely would not understand.

This required a female friend—one who could keep a secret. I had several local friends, women I'd known since school days, but they were all married, and their husbands knew, or in some cases were even good friends with, Don. I knew each one would promise not to tell their husbands, but I couldn't risk any word of my indiscretions getting back to Don.

The logical choice was my friend in Los Banos. She lived far enough away that even if she were to mention it to someone, they were unlikely to know me, and even less likely to care. The problem was in order to confide in her would mean revealing the real reason I'd visited her after such a long time, and that didn't feel right. She'd been so happy to hear from me when I called her, I didn't want to spoil her happiness now by admitting I'd had an ulterior motive in contacting her, even if it was the truth.

There was one other possibility, however: Amy.

Amy and I had been best friends in high school, but we'd grown apart afterwards, what with her getting married and me going off to college and then getting the job in the city. Even after I'd come back to Masons Flat we'd hardly seen each other. She and her husband, Gary, did come to our wedding, but it wasn't long afterwards that Gary left her. After that, Amy gradually dropped out of all the social circles in town. We saw each other occasionally, mostly when we'd accidentally bump into each other in the small grocery store or when she'd come into the butcher shop. When we did, we were always polite, saying it had been too long since we'd caught up, but neither of us had ever acted on our promises to plan a get-together.

I thought again about what good friends we were in high school. We'd always eaten lunch together, and did our homework together after school. Neither of us had been involved in many after-school activities, although Amy had been on the softball team for a while.

Would now be a good time to try to rekindle our friendship? After all, we'd been close. So close, in fact, that Amy had told me a huge secret—one I'd never divulged to anyone. Didn't that make her the perfect candidate for my secret?

I remembered the day as if it were yesterday. Amy had come to school looking as though she hadn't slept at all the night before. She barely said anything all morning and then, at lunch, we'd gone outside to sit on our favourite bench in the school yard, and after I'd asked what was wrong several times, she'd finally confided that her father's best friend had molested her the night before. The incident itself was horrific, but what had upset her even more was when she'd tried to tell her mother about it, her mother had grounded her for lying and had threatened to beat her black and blue if she said anything to her father or anyone else. Amy cried as she told me the story, so I knew she was telling the truth.

I think she regretted telling me though, and swore me to secrecy. She raced home quickly after school every day for a month after that.

We never spoke about it again.

And I'd never said a word to anyone, ever, about her secret.

What would Amy think about my confession? Would the bond we'd shared in high school still be strong enough to trust her with this? Would the fact I had honoured my promise never to break her confidence be enough to ensure she'd keep mine?

I went back and forth for three days. Firstly, trying to decide if she'd be likely to keep my secret, and secondly, if the fact that her husband left her made her a better or worse person to speak to. In the end I simply knew if I didn't talk to someone soon, I'd go nuts. Finally, I picked up the phone and called her.

She'd sounded surprised, but not unhappy, to hear from me. We agreed to meet in the parking lot at Lookout Park, mid-way between our homes, where we could take a stroll while we chatted. She'd seemed rather interested when I explained I needed some advice.

We met at ten-thirty on Sunday morning. Don had gone bowling with his friends as he sometimes did on a Sunday, so I never even had to mention to him that I was going out, let alone who I was meeting.

As I'd hoped, there were no other cars in the parking lot at the base of the small mountain, suggesting we could be lucky and not even run into anyone. I sat in my car until Amy arrived, and was surprised to see her turn up on a bike. Her cheeks were rosy from the exercise, and she looked genuinely pleased to see me. After our initial greetings, we began to make our way up to the lookout, following the least rocky of the trails. It wasn't particularly steep, so we were able to talk easily as we walked.

'I'm glad I finally made the call, Amy. It's been far too long since we've done anything other than say hello in the street.' I looked across at her, giving her a broad smile.

She glanced back at me for a moment and then looked down at the trail again before she spoke, her voice low and apologetic. 'Yeah, I ... I've thought about calling you a few times, too, but it never seemed like the right time, you know?'

I shrugged. 'I know what you mean. I was thinking ... a few of the girls from school are planning on starting up an arts and crafts group.

We'd meet once a week, and try different things every few weeks, with each member of the group being responsible to research something and then teach it to the others. I think the first few weeks they want to focus on crocheting baby blankets. But someone mentioned oil painting, and another said they'd always wanted to learn to do macramé. Does that sound interesting?'

A look of panic crossed her face. She bit down on her lower lip before answering. 'I ... I don't think so. They'll want to know about Gary—details, about why he left—and to be honest, it's not something I'm ready to talk about.'

I nodded, trying not to frown as I answered. 'I understand, but perhaps that's all you'd have to say. That you're not ready to talk about it?'

'No,' she said, shaking her head. 'It's not only that. It's also ... you know all I ever wanted was to be a wife and mother, right? I wanted three children. So did Gary. Or at least, that's what he told me when he proposed. But then he started saying we weren't quite ready yet, that he wanted to get his promotion and the salary increase that went with it, and he kept putting it off until ... well, you know what happened. So now, the thought of making baby blankets ... I couldn't do it.'

'I'm sorry you had to go through all that.'

'I am trying to put it behind me, but I'm sure not ready to make baby blankets for other people.'

I thought about suggesting she join later, when we did the oil painting, but I didn't want to press her too much. I wasn't sure where to go with the conversation, so I just blurted out my thoughts. 'Don wants children. And I suppose I do too ... sort of. I mean, it was a hard choice for me to give up my career, so having made the choice I guess it would be a waste if we didn't have a family.'

I heard her huff out a breath, and when I turned to look at her, her eyes had narrowed.

'I can't even begin to relate to that. All I ever wanted was to be a wife and mother—and I would have been great at both.' She stopped for a moment, looking off into the distance. Then she turned back to me, her face harder. 'There's no way I want to hang out with a group of women who only want to talk about their children and husbands. Get it?'

'Oh, of course. Sorry,' I said, internally chastising myself for my stupidity. She was still hurting and hearing them chatter would just keep the loss fresh in her mind. And my mentioning Don wanting kids probably hadn't helped either. 'You're right, they do go on and on about their little darlings—even I find it exhausting sometimes.'

I don't know how I hadn't realised this. She'd been devastated, and that was why she'd kept to herself so much. And here I'd gone and admitted what a hard decision it had been for me, choosing marriage and motherhood over the career I'd studied for. We really didn't have much in common any longer after all.

We continued to walk along in silence until we reached the lookout at the top, and then we made our way to a bench. We sat, admiring the view for several minutes, and then Amy turned to me with a quizzical look on her face.

'You know, it's been real nice catching up and all but, I'm curious ... why now, after all this time?'

My stomach started churning as the intuition which had been niggling at the back of my mind grew stronger until I suddenly regretted contacting her. This was a woman whose husband had left her for another woman, and even though I'd known that, somehow, I hadn't, until this very moment, considered exactly how that could impact her view on what I had to say. Would she, for example, have forgiven Gary if he'd told her about his affair and sought her forgiveness? Or would she have thrown him out? If I were to tell her what I'd done, would she laugh, saying something along the lines of all men have it coming? Or would she take the opposite view, that everyone who cheated was a horrible person? If it was the latter, this could go horribly wrong. Perhaps it was foolish to have thought she'd be a good person to talk to.

I had to say something, but what? I shifted on the bench until I faced her, forming a weak smile. When she smiled back, I swallowed hard, and something made me ignore all my doubts.

'I needed someone to talk to, Amy—a sounding board if you like—and I need some advice. You see, I've been unfaithful to Don, and I don't know what to do about it.' As I finished speaking, I watched her reaction carefully.

At first, her face was blank—devoid of emotion—but then her brow creased into deep furrows, making her look much older than her twenty-eight years.

She opened her mouth to speak, but instead she pursed her lips, clearly deep in thought. When she finally spoke, she practically spat the words at me. '*You* cheated on *Don*?'

I shrugged, feeling my face redden as I nodded yes.

'Wow,' she said in a tone that didn't hide her disbelief. 'I thought it was possible you'd found some clues suggesting he was seeing someone. I thought that might be why you wanted to catch up—thinking we had that in common. I'd thought you might be wondering if I'd suspected anything about Gary's affair before he told me about it. But, wow, you cheating on Don. I never saw that coming.'

When she first started speaking, I thought she was merely surprised because she figured she and I were similar and might, therefore, have had comparable experiences with our marriages. But then I recognised the look on her face. It was disgust. I stared at her, swallowing, unable to find my voice. She shook her head, still glaring at me.

'You do know I had a big crush on Don all through high school, right? I mean, God knows I tried not to let it show around you, but he knew. He knew, but he didn't care because he only had eyes for you. I think Gary knew too, but he wanted to marry me anyway. I thought Gary was so much in love with me that my high school crush on Don didn't matter, but I'm not sure now. Maybe the knowledge festered in him or something. All I know is he threw it all back in my face when he left, saying that was what drove him to the comfort of other arms.'

'And did you think ... I mean, if he'd asked for forgiveness would you have ... could you have?'

Amy threw her head back and laughed for a moment. Then her face darkened and her voice came out low and menacing. 'He didn't want my forgiveness. I don't think he cared one way or the other about my feelings. He simply wanted a divorce. He packed his clothes and left.'

'I'm really sorry, Amy, but ... it's not the same. I don't want to leave, I ... I just don't know how I can stay.'

Her eyes narrowed. 'What do you mean you don't want to leave? Do you think you can have your affair on the side, and still keep your marriage? Are you nuts?'

'No ... I mean ... maybe. It's ... complicated. I love Don, but this ... affair, as you call it ... it's like it was meant to be.' As I said the words out loud, I realised how bad it sounded, but it was too late.

Now she laughed. 'Oh, Evie, everyone thinks this new man or woman they meet is *the one*. That they'd made a big mistake when they got married, and their new lover is the one they were truly meant to be with.'

Her words struck me like a fist to the gut. Could that be what had happened with me? It couldn't be, could it? I'd never considered my marriage a mistake. And I still loved Don—that was the whole problem. If I didn't, I would just leave him and run off with Andrew. I wouldn't need advice. 'But I still love Don ... that's the problem ... that's the confusion I'm facing.'

She laughed again. 'You really are something, Evie. If you love Don, why did you cheat on him?'

I blinked a few times, hard. 'I ... never meant for it to happen.'

Amy shook her head, looking off into the distance. Her voice stayed even when she spoke. 'I don't know why you told me. I don't know what you expected me to say. Were you looking for some sympathy? Or for someone to tell you it was okay for you to cheat on the nicest guy for a hundred miles? I hope he leaves you.'

I stared at her, dumbfounded, at a complete loss for words. She still didn't look at me, however.

When I said nothing, her expression changed to one of surprise, and finally she looked straight at me. 'Wait, he doesn't know yet, does he?'

I licked my lips nervously. This was not at all how this conversation was meant to go. I'd hoped she would listen, express sympathy at my dilemma and, with a bit of luck, offer some advice. I shook my head, feeling utterly lost.

'All I can say, Evie, is you're a fool. Geez, he was on the football team and you were ... a nothing, a nobody, just like me. You were lucky to get him, and what have you done but thrown it all away.'

Her words stung. She didn't think I was good enough for Don. I'd never thought of it that way, but maybe she was right. He deserved so much more.

She huffed out a breath, her mouth open for a few seconds before she continued. 'I can't believe I trusted you with my secret all those years ago. I mean, if you're so untrustworthy that you've cheated on your husband, who knows how many people you told about my problems?'

I shook my head vigorously. 'No one, I promise. I never told a soul. That's why I felt I could trust you with this. I never betrayed your trust in me. I would never ...'

She raised a brow, giving me a wicked smile. 'You would never? What, you mean, like you'd never cheat on your wedding vows? That kind of never?'

Fear began to creep up inside me, making me shake. I was incredibly stupid to have ignored my intuition—to have trusted her with this knowledge. I had to quickly ensure this conversation would go no further, and that she wouldn't run to Don with the information.

'I've never told a soul, Amy. And I expect the same from you. You might be mad at me right now, but we owe it to each other to keep our secrets. Please. Don't tell anyone.'

She huffed out another breath, this time louder than the last. 'Oh, I would never tell anyone. Don't worry. I'm not like that. You just worry about yourself, and how you're going to fix your marriage.'

She turned on her heel and headed off down the track without looking back.

When I reached my car, she was already gone.

~~*~~

It had been almost two weeks since I'd spoken to Amy, and ever since I'd gotten home, I'd tiptoed around looking for any indication that Don knew something. Thankfully, it seemed, Amy kept her word. Don's demeanour around me hadn't changed one bit. I hoped my demeanour around him hadn't changed either, but I feared it couldn't be the case.

It had been nearly a month since the day I'd met Andrew in Modesto, and I was getting more anxious to see him every day. Unfortunately, Don hadn't been nearly as taken with the sourdough bread as I'd hoped he would be, so I hadn't been able to use that as an excuse for a trip back to Modesto. I struggled through each day, trying to think of an excuse to disappear for a morning or an afternoon, but came up with nothing.

Now and then, memories of Andrew's suggestion, saying I should go live on the beach with him in Santa Cruz, played on my mind. I fantasized about what it would be like to wake up beside him every morning and then follow him down to the beach to watch him surf. Maybe I would go for a run along the wet sand, the wind blowing through my hair, the salt spray tickling my face. It was what got me through some of the days—remembering he'd suggested it and convincing myself he'd been serious.

The nights were the worst. I had to pretend to enjoy what had become our nightly ritual. Don hadn't been kidding when he'd said he wanted a house full of kids, and he was determined to see me become pregnant. Every night I closed my eyes and thought of Andrew as my husband pressed into me. The best thing I could say about the whole experience was that at least it never lasted long.

Doubt about the connection I'd felt with Andrew tortured me, as did Amy's words. What had she said? Something about how everyone thinks the new man or woman is *the one*. Had I fooled myself into believing I meant more to Andrew than I actually did? After all, we hardly knew each other, so how could it be real? We had chemistry as well as our chosen careers in common, but were those things enough?

And I loved Don.

Didn't I?

I believed I did. Otherwise, it would be easy. Otherwise, there would be no dilemma.

The thought of hurting him was something I couldn't bear. Surely that drove my need to be so secretive, right? So that Don wouldn't get hurt?

I continued to wrack my brain for excuses to go to Modesto, but nothing sounded genuine.

And then, the following morning, I began throwing up.

~~*~~

As I drove to Sonora, I wondered how it could be that I hadn't noticed I'd missed my period. Had I been so distracted with trying to find an excuse to get away to see Andrew that I'd failed to pay attention to the days? Was I that much of a scatterbrain?

Nothing made sense. Not the affair. Not my lying to my husband. And not noticing something which should have set off alarm bells the moment I was two days late.

I parked, and made my way to the pharmacy, crossing my fingers that I wouldn't run into anyone I knew. When the coast seemed clear, I went inside, found the correct aisle, grabbed what I was after and headed to the cash register to pay. I thought I'd escaped, but as the girl at the register handed me my change, I heard my name spoken from somewhere behind me.

'Evie? I thought it was you,' said a woman's voice.

I turned, and there right behind me stood Debbie Dawson. Not only was Debbie one of the worst gossips in Masons Flat, she was also married to Carl, who happened to be one of Don's best friends. Running into her had to be just about the worst scenario imaginable.

'Debbie,' I said, forcing a smile onto my face, 'how nice to see you.' I shoved my change and the small parcel into my purse, hoping she hadn't noticed what I'd bought.

'Was that ...?' Debbie asked, her voice trailing off as her face clearly displayed disappointment that I had tucked my package away so quickly.

I shrugged, shaking my head. 'What?'

She lowered her voice to a whisper. 'Was that a pregnancy test kit? Because if it is, how wonderful. I know you and Don have been trying for some time now.'

Her tone of voice said it all. She wanted to be the first to know, so that once word got out she could tell everyone she already knew.

'Oh, that. Um ...' I was stuck. She'd seen it, so I saw no point in lying. 'Yes, but please, don't say anything to anyone. I don't want to get Don's hopes up, you know?'

She tilted her head as a frown creased her brow. 'Oh, okay. I mean, I think I'd tell my husband if it were me, but sure, okay. Your secret is safe with me.'

Again, I forced a smile onto my face. 'Thanks, Debbie. Knew I could count on you,' I said, wanting those words to be true but knowing they were as far from the truth as possible.

'You know, we should get together for dinner one night. Maybe we could go to the Masons Hotel or even the Italian place over in Angels

Camp? Carl and Don see each other every week, but I don't even remember when you and I last caught up.'

I remembered—too well. It was when Don's bowling team won the competition and the whole team went out with their wives and girlfriends to a restaurant in Angels Camp. Debbie had gotten pretty drunk and her tendency to gossip had gone completely unchecked. Any wonder she didn't remember—her subconscious didn't want to admit how horrible she'd been.

'Sure, that'd be fun,' I said, hoping it sounded genuine.

'I don't suppose you'd like to grab a cup of coffee or something right now?' she asked. 'Just let me pay for these things first.'

'Oh, it would be nice, and it was really great seeing you, but I'd better run. Busy afternoon you know. But let's do that dinner one night. Soon.'

After we parted, I raced out the door and to my car, and then sat for a moment catching my breath. I'd planned to use the restrooms at the shopping mall to do the test, but didn't dare now in case Debbie turned up there as well. Instead, I drove to a gas station, asked the attendant for the key to the restroom, and walked as calmly as possible around the corner.

When the test showed positive, I sat down on the lid of the toilet and put my head in my hands.

I expected tears, but none came.

Was I in shock?

Don and I weren't using any sort of birth control, so the child would be his, right?

I knew I was grasping at straws. We'd been having unprotected sex for three years. Why would I suddenly get pregnant now? Was the likelihood of a faulty condom stronger than the likelihood Don's sperm count had suddenly increased? Or that I had simply become more fertile for some reason? Nausea which had nothing to do with morning sickness washed over me, and my hands began to feel numb.

Had Andrew and I used a condom every time? For the life of me I couldn't be certain we had.

I could think of no one to talk to. I most definitely could not confide in Amy again—not after her reaction to just hearing that I'd cheated. And I couldn't say anything to my mother—while some wives might be trusted not to tell husbands, my mother wasn't one of them. If I told her, she'd tell my father and he'd tell Don.

And if Debbie knew we were trying to have a baby, it could only be because Don had mentioned it to Carl and Carl had mentioned it to Debbie. Talking to her about it would practically be the equivalent of contacting the San Francisco Chronicle.

Once again, I thought about ringing my friend in Los Banos. I came close to making the call this time, but even though I could trust her not to tell Don, I still couldn't bring myself to admit to her the real reason I'd gone down to visit her.

No, this was something I had to work through on my own.

Or was it? I could tell Andrew. After all, didn't he have a right to know? Besides, he might have been in a similar situation before and might have some ideas of what I should do. Then the thought of hearing him suggest I get an abortion hit me, and it terrified me.

Even so, wasn't it something I had to consider?

I walked over to the payphone just beyond where I'd parked and rang the number he'd given me. It rang three times and then a woman answered.

'May I please speak to Andrew?'

'Oh, I'm sorry; Andrew is no longer with us. I'm Cynthia Banks, and I've taken over his role. Can I help you with something?'

I could barely catch my breath, let alone form coherent words. Finally, I stammered, 'Oh, no thank you, it was ... it wasn't anything important. I'll, um, catch up another time.'

'Well, if it's a work matter, please don't hesitate to call me on this number.'

Struggling to compose myself, I answered her in the most professional voice I could muster. 'Thank you, Cynthia. I'll get back to you if I can't sort it out myself.'

I hung up the phone as an even stronger wave of nausea hit me. I raced back toward the bathroom, but threw up before I could get there. Thankfully, I hadn't eaten much today so there wasn't a lot to it. Wiping my face and pushing back tears, I ran back to my car and drove off.

I knew Andrew wouldn't have left without letting me know how to contact him. I had to get to Modesto to check the post office box, but I'd already been away for over an hour. Don would give me the third degree about where I'd been if I didn't get back soon. I began to sob uncontrollably, but then it occurred to me I could use Christmas shopping for my father as an excuse—after all, there was a large hunting and sporting supplies shop in Modesto.

When I mentioned it the following day after the morning rush had finished, Don frowned at first but then shrugged. 'Yeah, I can manage without you for a few hours. It's a bit early to be doing Christmas shopping though, don't you think?'

'It is, but if I can't find what I'm thinking of I'll need time to rethink. He's getting up there in age, you know, and he's got just about everything he could ever want.'

Don nodded. 'He has been talking about getting a new hunting rifle, but I'm not sure what he has in mind.'

I laughed. 'I am not getting my father a rifle. I was thinking something more along the lines of a fishing pole and all the stuff that goes with it. Then I could encourage him to take life a bit easier, and spend some time alongside a lake, you know?'

Don smiled and kissed my forehead. 'That sounds like a great idea. You're a good daughter. Drive safely.'

I made the trip in no time, arriving at the post office well before the lunch hour, then stood there gazing at the large wall of boxes not knowing which one was ours. Thankfully, I don't think anyone was paying any attention to me.

Eventually, I found the right one, and when I opened it, there was one envelope inside. I retrieved it and raced back to my car to read it in privacy.

The letter was written in the same elegant handwriting Andrew had used when he'd given me his phone number. It was addressed to Andrew Fletcher, at the post office box, and underneath the address it said *For Eve*. The return address was in San Diego.

There was a photo in the envelope as well, of Andrew at the beach holding his surfboard. Longing washed over me as I stared at the photo of the man who meant so much to me.

Finally, I tore my eyes from the photo to read the letter.

My Dearest Eve,

I hope this letter finds you well and happy.

While my health is as fine as ever, I have to admit to not being terribly happy. My sister hasn't responded to the treatment they gave her. The doctors don't give her much time.

I think I mentioned her two daughters? She's arranged for me to be their guardian, so I'm moving to San Diego. I'm not sure if it will be a permanent move, but I suspect things with her ex-husband may get messy, so I don't expect to be able to take the girls out of the area.

I wanted to see you in person—to hold you, and tell you how much I love you, and to beg you to come with me. I've never felt this way about anyone I've ever known. I would do everything in my power to make you happy if you could see yourself with me.

I'll be staying at my sister's house to keep things as easy for the girls as possible. The phone number at the house is at the bottom of this note. Please let me know you got this and that you'll give some thought to coming down. I know it's a lot to ask of you—to leave your husband and your family—but I also know that we are meant to be together. Please call me.

All my love,

Andrew

CHAPTER 11

Present Day

Taylor's visit with the commercial kitchen supplier proved to be more successful than she'd dared to hope, and in just over an hour she'd purchased the ovens she wanted, received a good discount on them, and was even promised they could be delivered with forty-eight hours' notice.

She looked at her phone's navigator, and planned out the short drive to Old Sacramento where she was meeting Casey for lunch. Some fifteen minutes later she'd parked and, with over an hour to kill, decided to walk along Front Street and take advantage of the glorious weather. She made her way past restaurants and shops until she spotted where they were to meet—the same restaurant where she and her sisters had lunched the day they'd come into Sacramento to do some Christmas shopping last December.

After a half hour, with still another half hour before Casey would arrive, she decided to go back and re-read the letter. Standing beside the car, she pulled the letter out and read it slowly this time.

The letter made it clear Andrew was in love with this woman named Eve. But who were they? And why would a letter addressed to a woman in Modesto be hidden under the floorboards of a butcher shop in Masons Flat? She pulled out the photo and studied it, wondering about the handsome man and the mysterious woman who had caught his eye.

The letter also made it very clear that Eve was married.

And had a family.

Did that mean she had children?

At the thought, Denver's words about faithfulness hit her squarely in the chest. This woman, whoever she was, had been cheating on her husband. Taylor searched her own heart for answers, but struggled to imagine any circumstances that would make her cheat on a husband.

She pulled out her phone and checked the time. Casey would be arriving in a few minutes, so she returned the letter to the box. She considered bringing it with her to show Casey, but an inner voice told her to protect it from prying eyes so she put it back in her car, and began the short walk to the restaurant.

She met Casey in the foyer and within minutes they were shown to a table. Taylor wondered if it might even be the same table where they sat last time, only now, with the warm weather and the sun glistening on the river below them, the location was magical.

After they ordered, Taylor gave Casey an update on the progress with the bakery, and then casually mentioned her date with Denver.

'You went on an actual date? That's great news, isn't it? You seem a little ... unsure.' Casey cocked her head, her brows coming together in a quizzical frown.

'It was nice. He's really ... nice,' Taylor answered, not surprised Casey had suspected something wasn't right.

'Ahhh. *Nice,*' Casey said, dragging out the word before she looked across toward the river for a moment. When she turned back to Taylor, she shrugged. 'Well, I suppose it was a lot to ask. I mean, Alex and Travis, me and Nick ... it probably is too much to think you and Denver would actually work out as a couple.'

'I was thinking the exact same thing. I have to wonder ... if I hadn't gone back to Melbourne, if I'd stayed here all along, would our friendship have developed into something more? I don't know. But now it seems ... a bit forced or something.'

'Hey, if it's not there, it's not there. You know how much I've always relied on chemistry. It was always there with Nick, we just got off to a bad start that first night.'

'Yes, I remember,' Taylor said, trying to control a grin.

'Don't force things with Denver, but don't close the door either. Who knows, maybe you two are simply experiencing a slow-burn rather than fireworks.'

Taylor nodded, again trying to conceal her grin, but Casey must have seen it.

'What are you grinning about, Taylor Mason? I wouldn't have thought this situation with Denver was something to be smiling about.'

Taylor shook her head. 'No, of course it isn't. That's not ... look, it's just when you said about chemistry ... well, there's someone else. And there's a lot of chemistry with him.'

Casey's head dropped, and she looked up at Taylor with a quirked brow. 'Okay, spill it. Don't keep me in suspense.'

Taylor laid it out: meeting Grant the first day, watching him surreptitiously as she cleaned the window, the reactions in her body when he stood next to her—as though he was stealing all the oxygen from the room—and the tingles she'd felt as she'd watched the way his muscles rippled as he'd worked.

'Wow. He sounds yummy,' Casey purred.

When the waiter arrived, they both sat back, allowing him to place the food on the table, but the moment he left, Taylor continued, telling Casey about how Grant had turned up at the bar in Sonora.

'Wait ... what? Denver invited him to come along ... on your date?'

'No, not exactly. Denver had told him about the band, is all. Him, and some girls he knew from his school days. He knew how good the band was, and wanted others to know they were playing there.'

'Oh, I see. Well, that's okay, right? I mean you had dinner first, so I suppose that was the date part of the night.' Casey said, the furrows in her brow deepening.

'I guess. We did have a lovely dinner, and then we went to the bar. That's when it all sort of ... fell apart.'

'Hmph,' Casey said, 'can't say I've ever had a guy do that before. But tell me, when he dropped you home, did he say anything about having another date?'

'No.' Taylor tried to remember his exact words. 'Not exactly, but he wouldn't let me pay for my share of dinner, so I'd said it would be my shout next time and I remember saying I'd had fun and was looking forward to reciprocating. And then we, sort of, said goodnight.'

'Well, I think if it were me, I'd take things slowly with both of them. Give yourself time to sort out your feelings, see which one of them makes the next move. This Grant chap does sound interesting. And did you say you danced with him?'

'No, he danced with one of Denver's friends though, and I was mesmerised watching them.'

Casey took a sip of her drink, and turned to look out over the river again. When she turned back, she shrugged. 'Take things slowly. That's all I've got. Sorry.'

Casey was right. She had to take her time getting to know both of them, but also be careful not to lead either of them on. This was definitely new territory—two men paying attention to her at once.

They finished their meals while Casey chatted about her new job. Then she mentioned the song she was working on, about Daisy, their great-great-aunt who'd moved to San Francisco and had written letters to her sister, their great-grandmother. It was Daisy's letters that Casey had stumbled upon a few weeks before Christmas.

And as soon as Casey said Daisy's name, Taylor remembered she wanted to talk to Casey about Eve's letter.

'You know, you're not the only one to find old letters,' Taylor said, raising a brow as she gave her mischievous grin.

'What do you mean?' Casey asked.

'Well, letter anyway, not letters. I found an old letter.'

'And?' Casey asked impatiently.

'And it was inside a metal tin, roughly the size of an Anzac Biscuit tin, under the floorboards in what will be my office at the bakery.'

Casey's curiosity was clearly piqued. 'A hidden box. With a letter and ...?'

Taylor explained the contents of the box, including the photo.

'Interesting. And you say it was addressed to a woman named Eve?' Casey cocked her head, deep in thought, making Taylor wonder if she knew something.

'Yes, written by a man named Andrew,' she answered. 'Do you know who this Eve might be?'

'Maybe. I have this vague recollection ... it'll come to me.'

'I only found the box this morning. I might have to ask around to find out if anyone still lives in Masons Flat who would have lived there in the early 80s.'

'Nick's parents did. Oh, that's it! I remember Nick telling me something about an aunt of his who he never met. I'm pretty sure her name was Eve ... or actually, I think it might have been Evelyn but she might have gone by Eve. She disappeared before he was even born, but his father had talked about her a few times. Nick mentioned her when we were talking about Daisy's letters.'

'Seriously? You mean Eve, the woman in the letter, might be Nick's aunt? What a tangle of human tragedy. First Daisy, now Eve. What sort of families have we found ourselves mixed up with?'

Casey laughed, shaking her head. 'Let's not get ahead of ourselves. I could be wrong about the name. Let me talk to Nick tonight—I'd ring him now but he's in some all-day workshop thing today. Maybe I'm wrong about his aunt's name. It was just a quick conversation after all, and it hasn't come up again since.'

They paid the bill, and then walked to Taylor's car where she pulled out the box to show it and its contents to her sister. Casey picked up each of the trinkets and studied them, then read the letter with great interest.

'Do you mind if I take a photo of it to show Nick?' Casey asked.

Taylor was relieved that's all Casey wanted to do because she didn't think she'd be able to let go of the original letter. 'Sure. And take a photo of the envelope too.'

Casey pulled out her phone and snapped two quick photos. 'Okay, I'll talk to him tonight. If I am right, and Eve was his aunt, he'll be very interested in this.'

At two-thirty they said goodbye, and Taylor began the drive back to Masons Flat well ahead of any commute traffic. It was a long, but not unpleasant, drive in the old Buick that had been their uncle's car. It was comfortable, but its radio had seen better days so she didn't bother with it, which gave her plenty of time to think about both Denver and Grant.

When she arrived back in Masons Flat, she was no closer to resolving her predicament; but at least she'd made some progress with respect to the letter.

CHAPTER 12

1984 – Eve

I'd been thinking about Andrew's letter constantly. I'd driven to the gas stations in Angels Camp, the one in Sonora, and the one in Jamestown over the last few days, each time wanting to call Andrew, but each time I'd started to put money in the payphone something had made me stop. Was it because I suspected that if I told him about the baby, he'd talk me into going down to San Diego to be with him? Was I so weak that just hearing his voice would be enough to make me walk out on my entire life? Could I leave my husband, my parents and my brother behind to be with someone who I'd only had a brief affair with?

And even if I could find it in me to leave my family, wasn't Andrew's life complicated enough now? He had his nieces to look after, and a very ill sister. It couldn't be fair to dump this on him, too, could it?

As much as I yearned to be with him, I simply couldn't do it.

I loved my husband. I loved my family. And somehow, being forced to make a choice made me realise the importance of my life here in the town that had always been my home.

Yet if it was true, why did I still feel so torn?

Indecision continued to plague me for several more days, but while lying in bed one night, everything became clear. I was greedy. Exactly as Amy had said, I wanted to have my affair and keep my husband. I wanted the comfort of what I'd always known, and I wanted Andrew. The frustration came from being smart enough to know it wasn't possible. Life didn't work that way. I had to give up one or the other, and the sensible side of me knew Andrew was the one I had to give up.

The following morning, I tried to talk to Don. I wanted to come clean with him before I had the chance to change my mind, but telling your husband you'd been cheating on him, and that you might be pregnant with the other man's child, wasn't something that found its way easily into conversation.

A week later, after several more nights where I barely slept as my mind raced with further indecision, and still having not found the right time to make my confession, it dawned on me there would be no point trying to hide my pregnancy for very much longer. I'd always been slender and, while clothing choices would no doubt hide any weight gain from others for quite some time, Don was likely to notice it much sooner.

I waited until we were having a bit of a sleep-in on Sunday morning. Lying flat on my back and with him on his side looking at me, I smiled, raised a brow, and put my hands on my abdomen. He cocked his head, frowning at first, but then a hopeful smile lit up his face.

He reached over and placed his hands over the top of mine. When he looked up, there were tears in his eyes. 'Are you ... are we going to have a baby?'

Seeing his tears nearly broke my heart. 'Yes,' I replied, keeping my voice soft. I should have kept talking—should have confided everything right then—but I couldn't bring myself to do it. Instead, I gave him a half-smile and continued, 'but can we keep it a secret for now? Just in case, well, you know, in case anything goes wrong.'

He was so happy that I couldn't bear to ruin it for him. Or at least, that's what I told myself, even though I knew it had a lot more to do with me being a complete coward.

He pulled me close to his side and wrapped his arms around me. After a time, and in the comfort of his strong arms, I dropped back to sleep.

After that, with Christmas now only a few weeks away, everything got busy both at work and with our families, so we didn't talk about it much. We'd agreed not to tell the rest of the family until after Christmas, to avoid getting our parent's hopes up in case anything went wrong.

Thankfully, I didn't run into Debbie again after the terrible day in Sonora. If she came into the butcher shop at all, which come to think of it she must have, I was either out or so busy with paperwork that I didn't see or hear her. I kept expecting her to call me to try to line up a dinner, but perhaps she hadn't meant it any more than I had.

I thought about Andrew at the oddest times, when something would trigger a memory of his smile or his touch, but I did my best to keep those thoughts to a minimum as it made me too sad. Even so, I kept wondering how his Christmas would go with his family—wondering whether his helping around the house might have given his sister a chance to improve, wondering how the girls were coping, and whether they were excited as Christmas approached. And then, it occurred to me that his sister might not have improved, and that they could already be in mourning for the loss of their mother and sister.

When Christmas was behind us, I knew I would soon run out of excuses why we shouldn't tell our families. That's when my panic refused to remain at bay.

Don, however, was over the moon. His brother had three children, and Don had always been jealous of that. He'd come close to telling him a couple of times, and had I not been standing there when he was on the phone with him, I'm quite certain he would have.

He didn't have to hide his excitement around me, however, so he'd started talking about turning the guest bedroom into a nursery, asking my opinion about what colour I wanted him to paint the walls and what sort of crib we should buy.

Sometimes his enthusiasm captured me, and we would discuss furnishings and even baby names. Other times, fear would wash over me and I'd have to feign a headache and go up to our bedroom for a rest.

On those days, with fear coursing through my veins with an icy chill, I'd sit with a calendar working back to the dates I'd been with Andrew. I don't know why I kept doing it because I always got the same answer. The most likely day I conceived was our anniversary—the day I'd spent one glorious hour in a Modesto motel room with Andrew.

And if that *was* the day, and if Andrew *was* the father, the baby could look like Andrew. What if he or she had caramel-coloured skin and curly dark hair? Genetics was a funny thing—I'd studied it a little in high school. The baby could take after my English and Irish ancestors, or Andrew's African ones, or if indeed Don was the father, he or she could take after Don's Nordic side of the family and have his blonde hair and blue eyes.

It was like rolling dice.

I could get lucky and Don might never know anything.

Or I could be very unlucky.

One thing I'd become certain of over the weeks since I'd received Andrew's letter, was that I couldn't leave. I loved Andrew. But I also loved Don. Just not with the same intensity.

But there was more at stake than my own feelings now.

I had no doubt that Don would make a wonderful father. My brother, Mark, had finally proposed to his girlfriend, Linda, and I knew they were planning to have children, so my child, and hopefully his or her siblings, would grow up surrounded by loving relatives. And my parents would be the best grandparents imaginable. I had to do what was right for my unborn child. That's how it had to be. I couldn't run off with a man I barely knew, to live in a city I knew nothing about, and throw everything else away.

I just couldn't.

I also couldn't run the risk of not telling Don because if the baby were to look like Andrew, the shock could be too much. Don would need time to process the possibility and prepare for it. I had to tell him, and hope he would understand and forgive me.

And if he couldn't forgive me, at least I could leave knowing I had tried.

~~*~~

The cold wind hadn't let up all afternoon, and we walked into a freezing cold house when we arrived home. Don went to light the fire while I changed from my work clothes. Shortly afterwards, I came down to start dinner.

I made one of his favourite meals, spaghetti with meatballs. When we finished eating, I stayed at the table.

'Do you want a hand with the dishes,' he asked, cocking his head.

I rarely wanted help but suspected he was confused by me still sitting after we'd finished as I generally jumped up straight away and cleaned up so I could watch a bit of television with him afterwards.

'No, that's okay. I just ... there's something we need to discuss.'

His face went pale. 'You're not sick are you? Or the baby? Please, tell me you're both okay.'

I shook my head. 'It's nothing like that.' I reached across the table and put my hand on his forearm. He smiled, and placed his other hand over the top of mine, giving it a gentle squeeze.

'What is it then, darling? What's troubling you?'

The concern in his voice nearly broke me, but I couldn't back down now. I had to tell him. Even so, though I'd practised the words over and over, I couldn't make them form in my mouth. I took a couple of deep breaths and swallowed hard. When a tear rolled down my cheek, his brows came together and he reached up and wiped my tear away. His kind gesture made it even harder. More tears fell.

'Oh, darling, nothing can be that bad. What is it? Is it something I've done? If so, I'm sorry. For whatever it was. Or have you scraped your car against a tree or something?' He tried to lighten the mood with a bit of a laugh, but I was in no mood to laugh.

'No, it's ... I feel dreadful, Don, and I'm not sure how to put what I've done into words.'

His face went paler still, and he withdrew his hand and placed both palms flat on the table. He nodded a couple of times, and then I saw his Adam's apple go up and down as he swallowed hard. 'Whatever it is, you should just come right out and tell me, because what I'm thinking is probably far worse than anything you could have done. Best to simply put it out there and not overthink it.'

I took a deep breath and crossed my arms in front of me, rocking slightly on the hard wooden chair. When the words finally came, they fell out of my mouth in a rush.

'I had an affair. It's over, and ... it was a terrible mistake, and ... I am so, so very sorry.'

The shock and pain that twisted his face was worse than I'd expected. I might as well have stabbed him with a kitchen knife. He looked away, then turned back to me and opened his mouth to speak, but said nothing. He stood, glared at me for a moment, then left the room. A moment later I heard the front door slam. Then I heard him come around the side of the house, and the kitchen door opened.

He stood there, fists clenched, face twisted with emotion. When he spoke, his voice came across as laced with pain. 'It was at that conference you went to in the city, wasn't it?'

I couldn't look at him as I tried to swallow the lump in my throat. I still didn't look at him when I finally got the courage to answer. 'Yes.'

'I knew you were different when you got back. You'd changed, but I couldn't put my finger on it. So ... did you see him again after that?'

I couldn't lie about it. Not now. 'Yes, twice more.'

He nodded, chewing on his bottom lip. Seconds went by. Maybe it was minutes. Finally, he sat down across from me. His eyes burned with both pain and supressed anger. 'And do you love him?'

I shook my head, and for the first time since all this had happened, I felt certain that my real love was for my husband. 'No, no, Don, I love you. I promise, it's just you. It's always been you.' I reached for his hand, but he pulled it away before I touched him, putting both his hands under the table.

'You don't love me the way I love you or you wouldn't have cheated on me. And you didn't do it just once, but three times. And so ... this baby ... is there a chance it might be his? Is that why you're coming clean with me now?'

He was right, of course. 'Yes.'

'My God, Evelyn, how could you do this to us?'

My tears began to fall again, and I shook my head back and forth. 'I don't know. I have no excuse. I was wrong. Terribly wrong, and I am so sorry. I will do anything in my power to make it up to you. Anything.'

He nodded again, and then began looking around the room. I'd never seen him this way and didn't know if he was going to cry or grab something to kill me. I couldn't tell which emotion was stronger.

'Have you told him about the baby? Is he interested in the child?'

I shook my head. 'No, he doesn't know anything about it, and I have no intention of contacting him again so I see no way he would find out. He's moved ... so there's no chance of me running into him.'

A laugh laced with anger erupted from him. 'Now I see what's going on here. He's moved away—is that a subtle way of saying he dumped you? And if he hadn't, you'd still be seeing him? Is that what you're saying?'

I had done so much lying, and felt so sick about it, that I had to come completely clean. If we were to try to make things work, I had to start being truthful and promise to never lie to him again.

'I tried to ring him to tell him I was pregnant. That's when I found out he's left. I won't be contacting him again. I promise you that. And he won't contact me because he doesn't even know where I live. He knows my maiden name, but I never told him where we live and he doesn't have any phone number for me.'

'We. So, he knew you were married, and yet he slept with you anyway.'

I shrugged. What could I say?

'I don't know, Eve. I really don't know what to think. I don't even know who you are anymore. If anyone had suggested you would cheat on me, I'd have said they were nuts, and that you would never cheat on me—not for anything. I'm still struggling to believe you've done this.'

So was I, if the truth be known. It had been so out of character, and maybe that was part of the thrill—doing something so utterly bad for the first time in my life. 'I love you, Don, and don't know what came over me. I can't even blame it on getting drunk, because that's not what happened. Maybe because he was exotic, or because he looked at me like I was special.'

'Wait.' Don stood up, his eyes becoming even harder. 'Did you just say he was *exotic*? In what sense?' His hand jutted forward and he pointed to my abdomen with disgust. 'What sort of baby are you carrying in there?'

I pushed my chair back and moved toward the staircase, crossing my arms over my abdomen. I felt threatened, for the first time since I'd known him, and I had a sense that I needed to run up to our room, lock the door, and protect my unborn child. Instead, I stood my ground and answered him. 'His father was African American, but his mother was French—Caucasian. He's got green eyes, but his skin is unmistakeably dark. Even if the child is his, which mightn't be the case, there's no certainty the child would be dark-skinned.'

His eyes became slits, and he nearly spat the words at me. 'You cheated on me with a black man? What the blazes ... Evelyn ... how could you do that to me?'

I began to shake, both out of fear for myself, and for my unborn child. I had never seen Don so angry, and as much as I thought I knew him, right now I truly had no idea what he might do.

'I guess that answers my question,' I said without meaning to say the words out loud.

He glared at me. '*YOUR* question?' he yelled. 'What question is that?'

'Whether you could love this baby even if it turned out he or she wasn't yours,' I said, my voice barely a whisper.

He ran a shaking hand through his hair, throwing dagger looks at me the whole time. Then he turned toward the kitchen door, cursing as he approached it. Finally, with his hands on his hips he turned to face me. 'I can't do this, Eve. If the baby is black, everyone will know you cheated on me, and that's not something I can live with. One of us should leave. Maybe it should be you ... or me, I don't know. I need time to think.'

He spun around and headed out through the kitchen door, slamming it behind him.

CHAPTER 13

Present Day

The front door was shut when Taylor pulled up at the bakery just after five. She knew it would be locked, but got out and tested it anyway.

As she stood surveying the quiet street, she wondered about the woman named Eve and whether she could indeed be Nick's aunt. One way or another, Eve must have worked at the butcher shop in order to have hidden that box. She didn't imagine it was common to see women butchers, but it didn't mean she couldn't have been one. Or perhaps her husband had been the butcher? With a bit of luck, Nick would be able to shed some light on this woman named Eve. If not, she could always speak to Sam over at the hotel. She didn't think he'd lived in town that long, but he seemed to know everyone in town so perhaps he could point her in the direction of someone who had.

With her head swimming with possibilities, she decided to walk across to the saloon and have a drink with Darleen. She knew Darleen hadn't lived in town long enough to have known Eve, so had no intention of mentioning the letter to her—she just wanted to think about something different.

When she entered, she was surprised to see Jeff and Denver at the bar, having a beer.

'Hey, madam baker extraordinaire,' Denver called out as she stepped inside, 'care to join us for a drink?'

'I'd love to, as a matter of fact. My shout?' she asked as she walked up and stood beside Denver at the bar.

'I won't have another, but thank you anyway,' Jeff said, finishing off the last of his beer. 'Gotta get home to the missus, you know? Oh, I mentioned the possibility of you giving her a job, and she's really excited. I'll bring in her resume as soon as she finishes it if that's okay?'

'Absolutely,' Taylor replied.

'You thinking of putting your wife to work in the bakery, are you Jeff?' Denver asked with a raised eyebrow.

'Yeah, we're thinking of starting a family one day, so it'd be nice to get ahead on the mortgage first, you know. In case I ever have lean months.'

'You? Lean months?' Denver said, reaching out and patting his friend on the back. 'Can't see that ever happening.'

'Hey, you never know what lies ahead ... none of us do. Anyway, I'm off—she's making a roast tonight. See you tomorrow?'

'I'll be there—seven-thirty,' Denver answered.

Once Jeff had gone, Denver turned to Taylor. 'So, how'd everything go with the supplier?'

'Great. They had ovens that are almost exactly what I've used at home, and they're in stock. And I managed to wangle a good discount, too.'

'Well done,' Denver said with a genuine smile.

Darleen walked up a moment later. 'When do you think you'll be opening up, Taylor? I've seen Jeff working over there for several days now, and that other big fellow. Another month?'

Taylor turned to Denver, then back to Darleen when he didn't answer. 'I hope it doesn't take too long, but until the work's done it's not done, if you know what I mean.'

'Oh, sure, there could be hiccups, but sounds promising. I can't wait to start offering some of your baked goods here at the bar. Now, I bet you'd like a lager, and Denver, same again?'

Darleen filled two glasses and slid them across the bar, then left to attend to a customer at the other end of the bar.

'Jeff mentioned he's done in the office, so I'll give Grant a call and get him to start in there tomorrow if that's okay? Did you pick out the paint you want?'

Taylor's hand flew to her mouth. 'Oh, I had a look at them but didn't take note of the name. Sorry.'

'It's no problem. Grant will need a day to get the walls ready anyway. There are bits of old wallpaper he needs to remove, and then he may need to do some patches in the plaster. So I can get the paint tomorrow and he'll probably paint it the following day.'

'Perfect. I'm thinking a soft, pale yellow might be good for the entire bakery—cheery, yet not obtrusive in any way.'

The smile Denver flashed her said it all. He couldn't care less which colour she chose, just so long as she gave him the name. 'I'll drop into the hardware store and look at colour charts again, then send you a text with the colour name.'

'That'd be great. So ... have you got plans for dinner?' he asked, his voice full of expectation.

'Casey and I had a huge lunch, so I'm thinking I'm not terribly hungry.'

Denver picked up his glass and drained the last of the pale gold liquid in one gulp. 'Okay, let me rephrase. Would you care to keep me company while I have dinner? You can have something light ... like a side salad or soup?' he asked as he ran the back of his hand across his mouth.

'I'd love to keep you company,' Taylor said with a wink.

'Great. Actually, I think one of Darleen's burgers and a serving of fries will do me. Is there anything here you'd like?'

She smiled, tempted to say she was looking at the one thing that she liked, because she really did like him so very much. She wished Grant hadn't come onto the scene to confuse things. Instead, she nodded and replied. 'I could probably manage a serving of those potato skins she does.'

~~*~~

'Have you got good news for me?' Taylor asked when Casey rang later that evening. She'd enjoyed sitting at the bar with Denver, munching on bar snacks, and had all but put Eve out of her mind while they'd eaten, but the moment she saw her sister's name, it all came flooding back.

'Yes, and no. I spoke to Nick, and I was right. His aunt was named Evelyn, but he doesn't know much about her. Just as I thought, she ran off before he was born and, her name rarely comes up in conversation.'

'Wow, so my Eve could be his Aunt Evelyn?'

'Seems likely, don't you think? Evelyn isn't exactly a common name.'

'No, it's not these days but it might have been back then. So, is he going to speak to his father?'

'Yes. He tried ringing him but it went to voicemail. He thinks his parents are probably out having dinner, so he said he'll try again in the morning. If your Eve is Nick's aunt, then his father will more than likely be extremely interested in whatever you've found.'

Tingles of excitement raced through Taylor at the thought of this being something important and not just a forgotten trinket box. If it was Nick's aunt, it could explain why she'd run off. She could have gone to live with her lover—Andrew—and simply not told any of the family. Maybe she knew her family wouldn't accept a black man. It was the eighties, so it should have been common enough by then, but perhaps not in a small town.

'You'll ring me as soon as Nick has spoken to him, won't you?' she asked.

'Of course. I'll let you know as soon as I hear anything.'

CHAPTER 14

1985 – Eve

I jumped at the bang of the kitchen door and then listened to his retreating footsteps along the porch. After a moment, I heard his truck start, followed by the crunching of the stones on the driveway.

When I knew he wasn't coming back, I returned to the table and sat with my head in my hands as his words continued to play over and over in my mind. *One of us should leave. Maybe it should be you.*

He was right. I should leave. I'd broken our vows, and he couldn't forgive me. And even if he could somehow find it in his heart to forgive me, there was no way he'd be able to live with the shame if the whole town knew I'd cheated on him.

I'm not certain how long I sat there, but eventually I trudged up the stairs to the guest bedroom and pulled a small suitcase from the top shelf in the closet, then headed to our room. After setting the suitcase on the bed, I stared at it for some time—allowing my mind to spin as I wondered where my tears were. My husband had just stormed out, and yet I couldn't even cry.

I felt numb.

Eventually I opened the suitcase, then gently folded some underwear, casual tops, skirts and sweaters, and placed everything inside. Thinking about my condition, and having no idea how long I might be away, I chose the loosest fitting clothing I owned. Then I retrieved my hidden stash of money from an old boot and counted it—three hundred and sixty-five dollars. It wouldn't last long, but it was something. In addition, I had one credit card in my name so I could use that if I needed to.

With the suitcase packed, I headed back downstairs and once again sat at the kitchen table, listening for any indication Don might be returning. There was nothing. No footsteps coming along the porch. No cars approaching. Nothing but silence.

I clenched and unclenched my hands several times, again replaying his final words to me. He was hurt, and rightly so. He'd stormed out of the house, but I suspected it had more to do with pain than anger. I'd hurt him—terribly. It was unsettling. And yet, I still didn't feel like crying.

Had I become a monster?

I knew I should get in my car and go look for him—it was the right thing to do—and sitting here wouldn't achieve anything.

I grabbed my purse and keys, and headed outside. He would have gone into town—perhaps the saloon or maybe even to the butcher shop to take out his frustrations on a carcass. I made the short drive and did two laps around Main Street and the surrounding streets. When his truck clearly wasn't anywhere, and there were no lights on in the butcher shop, I headed to Jamestown to check his second favourite drinking hole. A small town, it only took a few minutes for me to check the area to know he hadn't come here, either.

My mind continued to spin with memories of Don's words, as well as Andrew's suggestion that I should go to him in San Diego. Maybe that was the answer. I could drive to San Diego in two days. My stash of money would be enough to cover gas and a motel and a couple of meals.

I drove around the corner to the gas station and pulled up right next to the payphone. I sat for a few minutes, rocking back and forth as I tried to make up my mind. Eventually, I retrieved the tiny scrap of paper that held his new phone number.

'I got your letter,' I said to him when he answered. He sounded surprised to hear from me.

'Eve,' he said, his voice soft and low. 'It's ... so good to hear your voice.'

'Oh, Andrew, I've missed you so much. Is your sister ... is everything okay with you and your family?'

He sighed before answering. 'She's gone, but the girls and I are doing fine. It's been rough for them, but each day they are better than the last. But enough about me, how are you? It's so good to hear from you. I hoped you would call me. Is everything okay? You're not in trouble or anything, are you?'

I smothered a laugh. If only he knew. 'Everything is fine. Just on my own tonight and feeling a bit lonely. And as I said, I got your letter.' I hoped he couldn't hear any street sounds to give away that I wasn't calling from home.

'On your own? Is your husband out of town?'

Perfect question. 'Yes, he's gone away for a couple of days. Look, I probably shouldn't have called. I just ... I wanted to hear your voice. It's been ... so long. I wanted to know that what we had was real.'

I heard the puff of air as he let out a breath, and I could imagine the frown developing on his face. 'Of course what we had—what we *have*—is real. I think about you every single day. If there's anything wrong, Eve, come down here. The girls will love you as much as I do. I haven't changed my mind about us, not at all. It's been a rough couple of months, and thinking about you, and looking forward to seeing you again, has helped me hold it together.'

His words gave me so much comfort, knowing that if Don didn't come home, if his anger didn't subside, I definitely had somewhere to go. I swallowed hard, finding my voice.

'Thank you, Andrew. I miss you too. But ...' I sighed. How much could I say? How much *should* I say? The last thing I wanted to do was give him false hope, but at the same time I wanted to keep the option open now that I knew he still wanted me. Confusion had me tongue-tied.

'Look, just come here. Please. If money's an issue, I'll book a flight for you. How does that sound?' The desperation in his voice nearly convinced me to say I would go to him.

Finally, a tear fell. I chewed on my lip for several seconds, unsure what to say. Unsure if I should tell him everything. One side of me wanted to, but it didn't feel like the right thing to do. My stomach tightened with indecision. Only a few hours ago I'd all but made up my mind that I loved Don, not Andrew, and yet Andrew might soon become my only option. I hated not being truthful with Andrew, but for the baby's sake I had to keep my options open.

'Look, I ... I have to go. I'm sorry. I'll call you tomorrow ... or the next day. I shouldn't have called so late.'

As I pulled the handset away from my ear, I could hear him protesting, asking me to wait. But I couldn't keep talking to him. I couldn't tell him everything. Not yet. Maybe tomorrow it would make more sense.

~~*~~

I woke feeling as exhausted as I'd been when I'd finally drifted off to sleep.

It didn't help that I'd woken several times through the night, holding my breath as I'd listened; hoping that what had woken me was footsteps coming up the staircase. Each time it had been nothing more than the creaking of the old house or the wind rattling the windows.

When the alarm went off, I rolled over, hoping to find Don asleep beside me. Instead, his side of the bed was cold and undisturbed. I felt nauseous and would have preferred to stay in bed, but I got up anyway. People were counting on the butcher shop to be open. Don had worked hard to develop loyal customers, and I couldn't let them down.

Forcing myself up and out of bed, I made some toast, then took a quick shower, and headed into town.

It was busy from the moment I arrived, not unusual for a Friday. Luckily, being busy meant there tended to be several customers in the shop at any one time so no one tried to make much in the way of casual conversation. A few did ask about Don, and I simply said he was under-the-weather—no one seemed to doubt me for a moment. For that I was grateful, as casual banter never came easy for me. That was Don's specialty, not mine.

Thankfully, Don had prepared everything the afternoon before. It was something he generally did so as to be ready to serve people from the moment we opened. I'm glad yesterday had been no exception as I'm pretty sure I'd have had to draw the line at cutting anything up. I'm certain I would have lost my breakfast if I'd tried.

The other thing to be grateful for was that Debbie didn't make an appearance. I'd feared her arrival, feared her keen eye for gossip might see more in Don's absence than others did. I also feared that having had three children herself, there could be something in my demeanour that might give away the fact that I was indeed pregnant, and I did not want to discuss any of this with her.

When things quieted down in the late morning, I headed to my office hoping to focus on paperwork, but all I could think about was my brief conversation with Andrew. He wanted me. Why couldn't I just go to him? What was holding me back? Was it because I knew, deep down, Don would return? Because I trusted that his love for me would eventually overpower his hurt and anger? Each time I heard the front door open, I raced out, hoping it was him, only to find another customer had come in.

By early afternoon my lower back started to ache, and my feet felt like they had grown two sizes too big for my sneakers, so when the clock finally clicked to five, and there was no one in the shop, I locked up and headed to my car. Just before I started it, I remembered the box hidden under the floorboards in my office. I considered going back to grab it—I would need to take the letter and my precious belongings with me if I left—but the other side of me hoped that when I got home, it would be to find Don sitting at the kitchen table waiting for me. He would have spotted my suitcase and known I was prepared to leave. Maybe he would tell me he hadn't meant it when he'd said I should go. Maybe he would tell me everything would be fine—he would learn to love our child whether or not he was the biological father.

If that didn't happen—if Don didn't return—I could open up for a few hours tomorrow and grab my box before leaving. Yes. That was a much smarter plan than trying to drive in the dark anyway. I would give him tonight and then leave tomorrow if he didn't come home.

When I pulled up in front of the house, I sat in my car gazing at the dark house, anxiety making the muscles in my abdomen constrict and spasm. Don's truck was nowhere to be seen.

I took a deep breath as I got out of my car. I didn't look forward to another night like last night, but what could I do? I wasn't going to go out looking for him again. My only choice was to wait. If he didn't return, I would leave in the morning.

Tears of frustration burned behind my eyes. Don and I had only had a few fights over all the years we'd known each other, and none of them had lasted more than a few hours. But this, this was something completely out of the ordinary, and I really, truly, didn't know how to fix things.

Pulling myself together, I trudged toward the front of the house, listening to the crunch of the gravel underfoot. There were only six steps—it wasn't like I had to climb Mt Everest—yet in my exhausted state, it seemed almost unsurmountable. I grabbed the handrail and began the climb. When I made it to the top, I stopped and arched my aching back. After a few moments, I turned to my right to walk along the wrap-around porch to the side door. I would enter through the kitchen, as I usually did.

I placed my hand on the doorknob and gave it a slight turn. It didn't budge. Of course it was locked—I was foolish to even hope it mightn't be. Don wasn't here. I'd known that the moment I'd driven up.

A mixture of emotions drenched me—fear, guilt, loneliness, trepidation, regrets—but funnily enough, I didn't feel heartbroken. Was I a horrible wife? I must be, because everything that had happened was my fault.

I put my key in the lock and turned the handle, then pushed the door open wide. I flicked on the light and drew in a breath, but the only thing out of the ordinary was the suitcase—the one I'd packed the night before and left sitting beside the table.

Again, Don's words haunted me. *One of us should leave. Maybe it should be you.*

I turned my head slightly as I reached around and tugged the strap of my purse back up onto my shoulder, and in my peripheral vision I caught movement further along the porch. A second later, a figure emerged from the shadows. Dressed in dark clothing with a hood pulled up, his features were hidden, but it had to be Don. My heart thumped. Why was he standing out here in the dark? Why hadn't he gone into the house to wait for me to come home?

'Hey, what are you—' I asked as I turned to face him.

CHAPTER 15

Present Day

Taylor slept in, then after a leisurely breakfast and two cups of coffee, she showered and washed her hair, enjoying the luxury of taking her time in the morning—something that would disappear as soon as the bakery opened.

Her plans for the day were to stop in to see how Jeff and Grant were getting on, but afterwards she would head over to pick up her friend, Jenny Chambers, the woman who'd taught her how to make the best cherry pie she'd ever tasted. At the time, Jenny hadn't minded sharing her family recipe with the woman who was heading back to Australia, but she might have a different view now that Taylor would be selling her wares here in town. She'd speak to Jenny about it on the drive over to Angels Camp, where they were to meet Darleen and another friend, Linda, for lunch.

As she walked into the bakery, the bopping rhythm of country music met her at the door, music not dissimilar to what Tommy and the Tripods had played on Saturday night. Enjoying the beat, she sashayed toward the doorway of the small office where Grant, already stripped down to his singlet, was pulling old wallpaper off the south-facing wall. Instead of ear-buds today, there was a small radio sitting on the floor.

'Good morning, Taylor. You sure look pretty today. Lunch date?' Grant said from mid-way up the ladder, his eyes practically undressing her.

Aware of the cleavage that the summer dress she'd chosen might reveal, she pulled at the shoulders to lift the dress. 'How's it going in here? Denver thought you'd probably be able to get the walls finished by tomorrow?' She'd intentionally ignored his question, preferring to keep things businesslike this morning.

'Yeah, sure. This wallpaper is a bit tougher than I'd expected, but I'll get it off, don't worry about it.'

'Oh, I wasn't worried. You'll be careful with the floors though, won't you? I'm thinking I might keep the floorboards in here and just have you put a coat of varnish on them.'

Grant stepped down off the ladder, bringing him within an arms-length of where she stood. He bent down and switched the radio off. Suddenly, his presence felt too close and intimate, but she held her ground anyway. As he stood, he wiped his forearm across his face and then put his hands on his hips. 'Just in here? Do you mean to say you might replace the floors in the other areas?'

She looked down at the floor, studying the marks and dents giving it character. Then she looked up, meeting his eyes. 'I'm thinking about it, yes. The front seems in pretty good condition too, but the thought of what might have been on the floors where the butcher worked isn't too appealing. I'm thinking linoleum or some other new material ... something easy to keep clean.'

Grant stretched his arms behind him, pushing out his chest slightly in the process. As much as she tried to ignore his action, her eyes were drawn to his tanned muscular frame.

'Well, if it were my place, I'd be leaving the rustic floors. They sort of suit the area, you know?'

Her cheeks felt flushed as she looked back up at his face, knowing he'd been watching her the whole time. 'Yes, I do know. That's why I think I'll leave them as they are in the retail area and in here, just not in the back where I'll be cooking. In fact, I'm pretty sure they wouldn't meet hygiene standards in any case.'

The atmosphere in the small room thickened, and Grant's face darkened with what her intuition suggested was a hint of anger. Yet it made no sense. Why would he care whether she replaced the old floors? She brushed the sensation aside, figuring she had to be wrong about what she'd seen on his face.

'Well, I'll leave you to get back to it and just say hello to Jeff,' she said, taking a step back from the doorway. His eyes never left her face, however, and after two steps, she stopped. 'Unless there's something else?'

A slow smile pulled up the corners of his mouth. 'No, nothing. Unless ... no, it's not appropriate.' He shook his head, but he didn't move.

Intrigued, she felt her forehead crinkle and a brow lifted of its own accord. 'What's not appropriate?'

He licked his lips, drawing her eyes to them. Then, taking a step toward her, he asked, 'Unless you'd consider having dinner with me this weekend?'

He was so close she could have placed her hand on his chest if she'd wanted to.

'Dinner? As in ... a date?'

'Yes, I suppose it would be a date ... if you don't already have plans.'

She hadn't expected that. As much as the chemistry between them was driving her nuts, she hadn't thought of it as being reciprocal. She'd pretty much assumed he was the sort of man who made all women feel a bit weak in the knees. Even Cherise, whom Denver had said was a happily married woman, had melted in his arms on the dance floor.

Her mind quickly turned to Denver. What would he think about her having dinner with Grant?

'This weekend?' she asked, needing more time to process what he'd said. Did she want to have dinner with him? And if she did, what did it say about her feelings for Denver?

'Only if you want to. Hey, I didn't mean to make you feel uncomfortable. I mean, you're the boss, and that sort of makes me an employee, so maybe it's not appropriate,' he said, taking a step back.

Her head started to clear as his physical proximity lessened. 'No, it's not that. I'm just ... surprised.'

'The offer is there. You don't have to answer me right now. Think about it,' he said, turning back to the ladder and climbing up to where he'd been when she'd walked in.

'Oh ... kay ... I'll, uh, check my calendar and let you know,' she stammered as she took two further steps away from him.

When she looked up, Grant winked, but he said nothing further.

She hurried over to the far side of the room where Jeff sat on the floor, pulling some wires out of the wall.

'Hey, Jeff,' she said in as nonchalant a voice as she could muster. 'How's it going?'

Jeff looked up, his face fixed with concentration. If she had to bet, she'd have said he'd heard every word of her exchange with Grant, and he was simply pretending to be surprised she'd walked up. She hoped the distance had muffled their conversation.

'Everything is going fine, Taylor. How about you? Are you starting to feel like you're a local yet?'

'Hardly,' she said with a chuckle. 'Although I reckon once the bakery is open, I'll get to know everyone within cooee soon enough.'

'Cooee? That must be some of your Aussie slang, is it?'

'Yes ... sort of means everyone in the local area and surrounds, I suppose.'

'Well, I suspect you're right—once this place opens, they'll be coming from far and wide for freshly baked bread and desserts. The bread at the grocery store is almost always stale,' he said with a laugh.

'I hope you're right. I'm counting on it, actually, or my career here may be short-lived. Now, I best stop yakking and let you get back to work. I'll probably drop by again tomorrow, but feel free to call me if you have any questions.'

As she headed for the door, she fought the urge to look into the small office again, but without even looking, she'd have bet something rather substantial that Grant was watching her.

~~*~~

Taylor had just dropped Jenny back at her house after their lunch in Angels Camp when she heard the familiar ping of a text message coming through from Casey.

> *Nick spoke to his dad, Mark, and yes he thinks your Eve must be his sister. He's very curious to see what you've found so he's coming up there tomorrow and would like to take you to lunch. Say around mid-day at the hotel bistro? I gave him your number, and here's his. You don't need to ring or anything unless you can't meet at noon.*

CHAPTER 16

After a quick breakfast, Taylor headed across the road to Blue Gum Park for a long walk. The familiar sight of eucalyptus trees was precisely what she needed to help her think through the dilemma she faced over Grant's dinner invitation. One side of her wanted to go—their chemistry was stronger than anything she'd ever experienced before—but she had to consider her feelings for Denver. She liked Denver. A lot. And the last thing she wanted to do was jeopardise their blossoming friendship.

She followed the track down the hill, closing her eyes and breathing in the sharp scents of eucalypt and pine. From time to time she had to pick her way around piles of horse manure scattered along the track, and this made her wonder if Denver and Travis rode their horses through this park. Then she remembered Alex telling her about riding here once. What if she were to come across him riding right now? She'd never seen Denver on a horse, given he'd been in a cast the whole time she was here at Christmas, but Alex had said he was every bit as good a rider as Travis.

Maybe after she met with Mark for lunch, she'd pop over to visit Alex. And if Denver and Travis happened to be riding, she could wander over and watch. Not only would it be fun to watch them, it would also give her a chance to focus on her friendship with Denver. It would probably be the smart thing to simply stay away from Grant. After all, once the bakery opened she'd be so busy she'd barely have time to think about one man, let alone two.

Maybe that was the problem. She had too much free time—something that was pretty much foreign to her. After so many years of working long hours at the bakery in Melbourne, she suddenly had time to go out to lunch, and make trips to see suppliers, and watch tradesmen do their work.

And to think.

Think, far too much.

That had to be a huge part of the problem.

When she reached a level area in the park she stopped and pulled out her phone. It was only a bit after ten, but she had to get home, and then shower and get ready for her lunch date. She took a few deep breaths, shoved her phone back in her pocket, and began the climb back up.

She'd think about Grant's dinner invitation later.

Much later.

~~*~~

The tall, dark-haired man standing outside the door of the hotel had to be Mark Gold. The family resemblance to both Travis and Denver couldn't be missed—the strong jaw, the eyes so dark they were almost black, and the broad shoulders. Other than the smattering of grey in his temples giving away his age, he could be another brother. His own son, the fair-haired Nick, was the odd one out. He must take after his mother.

When she approached, he smiled. 'You must be Taylor?'

'Hi, Mr Gold,' she said, reaching out to shake his hand.

'Call me Mark, please,' he said, taking her hand and giving it a warm squeeze.

'Shall we sit?' she asked, suddenly feeling a need to take charge of their meeting.

'Yes. I've already spoken to Sam. We'll have that far corner table. It'll be much more private, assuming this place fills up for lunch, which I highly doubt to be the case.'

Taylor tilted her head, raising a brow. 'Oh, okay.'

'After you,' Mark said, indicating for her to head to the table.

Once seated, Taylor decided to cut straight to the point. She placed the cloth bag onto the table and started to pull the metal box out of the bag.

'Oh, let's order first, shall we?' Mark said, placing his hand over hers to stop her. 'They do a fabulous T-bone steak here, and I'm starving. Let's order, and then we'll have plenty of time to talk before the food arrives.'

He definitely wanted to be in charge, so she took a deep breath, picked up the menu, quickly scanned it and selected a Cobb Salad. Americans were so much better at salads than Australians, and this one, with its combination of bacon, avocado, chicken breast, eggs and tomato was no exception. Her mouth watered at the thought as she informed him of her choice.

Mark stood. 'I'll go find Sam and place our order. And can I get you a glass of wine?'

'I think I'll just have some mineral water, thanks.'

When Mark walked away in search of Sam, Taylor pulled the metal box out, put the cloth bag onto the floor, and took the top off the box. Looking at the items—the beaded fabric horse, the small wooden car, and the tiny stuffed cat with emerald green eyes—she realised how possessive she'd become of them. If he said Eve was his sister, would he expect her to give him the box and all its contents? She looked over her shoulder but couldn't see Mark, so she quickly put the box back into the bag on the floor. She'd let Mark tell her about his sister first, and then decide how much of the contents of the box she would share.

When Mark returned a few minutes later, she waited for him to speak.

'So, you think you may have found a letter addressed to my sister? Is that right?'

She nodded. 'Yes, in a box hidden under the floorboards of my bakery ... the building that used to be the butcher shop. The letter was inside. It was addressed to a post office box in Modesto, but it was marked to the attention of Eve.'

Mark frowned. 'She always did prefer to be called Eve, not Evelyn. But the post office box in Modesto doesn't make any sense to me. May I see the letter?'

Taylor reached down beside her, retrieving only the letter. She handed it to Mark.

Mark read the letter slowly. Then he read it a second time, his eyes flicking to the photo from time to time as he read. When he finished, and met her gaze, he'd changed. The confident, take-charge-manner he'd oozed from the moment she met him melted away, and it was as though the smattering of grey in his hair had doubled. He cocked his head, a deep furrow appearing between his brows. 'She was having an affair? My own sister was having an affair, and I had no idea.'

Taylor, unsure what to say, picked up her glass and took a long sip. When she put it down, she met his stare. 'It was probably not something she wanted you to know.'

He cleared his throat, but his voice was still rather hoarse. 'What else was in the box? Besides the letter?'

'Nothing significant. A few trinkets. Oh, and a small key—possibly to the post office box, now that I think of it.'

Mark nodded, but didn't speak as he let the revelation sink in.

'And you're certain this Eve would be your sister, Evelyn?' Taylor asked, matching his quiet tone.

'If you'd found this anywhere else, anywhere other than the butcher shop, I'd say it couldn't be her. But how could it *not* be her? She and her husband ran the butcher shop ... until she took off.'

'You say she took off. What made you think that?'

Mark frowned, and cocked his head. 'It was obvious. She was gone. Her car was gone. She'd taken a lot of her clothes and personal items with her. Of course she took off.'

Taylor swallowed hard, feeling Mark's raw emotions as much as hearing them in his voice. 'Tell me about your sister, I mean, if you want to.'

Mark drew in a long breath. Then, rocking gently in the chair a few times, he looked up. 'She was beautiful, my little sister. Evie. That's what I liked to call her. Evie. She was smart, way smarter than the rest of us. She went off to college and got an accounting degree, then worked in the city for a top accounting firm until Don finally talked her into marrying him. He pushed her to quit the job and come back here to Masons Flat. He'd bought the butcher shop business and wanted her to do the bookkeeping. I'm pretty sure Dad helped Don convince her—because he wanted her to do the books for the family business too. I felt sorry for her, being pressured to give up such a good job, but it wasn't my place to intrude, you know? Kind of wish I had, now.'

'I see. So she did work at the butcher shop. I figured she had to, to have hidden the box there.'

'Yes, as I said, she did all the books and helped at the counter when they were busy. Don was a good man—and a good friend. Everyone in town liked him. And everyone felt his heartbreak when Evie took off.'

'And ... where did you think she'd gone? Did it occur to you she might have been having an affair?'

'Evie?' Mark shook his head dramatically. 'No way, not Evie, no one would have thought she'd ever be having an affair. We figured she'd run off with this cult. I remembered her talking about them when she was at college. They were all over the campus, and she was really curious about them.'

That made no sense to Taylor. A fairly conservative, college educated woman, who worked as an accountant, running off with a cult? Why would they think that? She frowned. 'And ... what made you think she'd run off with them? Had they been seen here in town?'

Mark shook his head again. 'No, but Don said she had talked about seeing them in the city several times. She often came home on the weekends while they were dating ... both while she was going to college and then when she got the job in the city.'

'I see,' Taylor said. 'So, she worked in San Francisco, right?'

'Yes. She wanted to become a Certified Public Accountant, and to get qualified she had to have the experience in an auditing firm. But after she got it, Don convinced her that she'd proven what she was capable of but that what she really wanted was to come back home and get back to her own people. In some ways, I was surprised she gave it up so easily, but then again, she and Don were in love. And she'd always been a country girl when she was a kid—rode horses, and cooked a lot, and talked about having a family.'

Taylor tried to reconcile all that. A woman from this small town, breaks out, gets a university degree and lands what sounds like a high-profile job in the city, earns significant credentials, and then gives it all up to come back here to this small town to work with her husband and father, only to run away to be with a cult only a few years later? Wow, she had to have been one super-confused woman.

'And you were all sure at the time that she'd gone off with this cult?'

Mark rubbed his jaw, looking down at the table. 'Don was sure. He said she'd mentioned seeing them in the city a lot. And then there was something about the cult having a big presence in Oregon—Don said that she'd sounded envious when she'd talked about it. Don was heartbroken. She never contacted any of us, and there was no way for us to reach her. It wasn't like it is now. People didn't all have cell phones the way they do now.'

Taylor still couldn't come to terms with how out of character it seemed for a woman who'd worked so hard to achieve what Eve had.

'I don't get it ... so she just left? What, in the middle of the night or something?'

'Don said they'd had some angry words—about her getting close to thirty and they hadn't started their family yet—and then he'd gone to stay with a friend in Placerville, from memory. He said he'd needed time to think, but that when he got home on Sunday afternoon she was gone, and so were some of her clothes. He was still a bit angry so he didn't even care at first.'

'And did you, or Don, go to Oregon to look for her?'

Mark shook his head. 'No. Look, I figured she'd be back, you know? I figured a week or two surrounded by those hippie-types and she'd be back. Only the weeks dragged into months, and there was no word from her.'

'And her husband? Did Don try to find her?'

Mark shifted uncomfortably in his seat. 'I don't think so. Like I said, Don was mad at first, and then he got so busy, running the butcher shop on his own. Besides, I'm pretty sure he felt the same way I did—that she'd wake up to herself and come back. Only she never did. Don tried to manage the business on his own, but after about a year he gave up. He let the lease run out, shut the door and moved to Arizona to be near his brother.'

Taylor frowned, finding it extraordinary that no one had tried to find her. 'And even then, when she didn't come back, no one from your family went to Oregon in search of her?'

'Look, none of us knew where to start. And it wasn't uncommon back then, you know? People went off with these hippie-cult-groups and got sort of brainwashed. I always figured Evie would see through them eventually and come home. Guess I figured wrong. Although now, seeing this letter, makes me wonder if it was a cult she ran off with after all. She might have run off with this man, this Andrew fellow.'

Taylor wondered the same thing, but if Eve had run off to meet Andrew, why would she leave the box behind? Could she have simply forgotten about it? That seemed unlikely.

'And what did the police think?' Taylor figured they would have followed the lead of the husband and family.

Sam arrived with their lunches, temporarily interrupting their conversation. Smelling the steak made Taylor envious, but after the first bite she was pleased with her salad.

'So,' she said, picking up the conversation where she'd left off, 'what did the police have to say about her disappearance?'

'I don't think they knew. Not at first, anyway. No one saw any need,' Mark answered, his voice trailing off.

Taylor felt her brow tighten, but tried to keep her voice neutral. 'But they did get involved ... later, right?'

'Yeah, Don eventually lodged a missing person report, but I don't recall anything coming of it. Then, when my father died, Evie was a major beneficiary in his will, so the lawyers tried to trace her. I'm not sure what their search involved, so maybe the police did some investigating at the time.'

'Eve's father died ... and she still didn't contact anyone? Didn't that make you wonder?'

Mark shifted again only instead of looking uncomfortable he now looked a bit angry, as though he felt her question was an accusation of some sort. She tried again in a softer voice. 'It's just ... you'd think she would have contacted her parents at some stage, you know?'

'How would I know what happens to people who get caught up in cults? She never contacted us. Period. Never asked for help, or money, or called to see how her aging parents were getting along. When the lawyers couldn't track her down, her share of the estate went into a trust account. It's still there. It's not like I killed her to get my hands on her money.'

Now it made sense—his change to a defensive position. Someone, at some stage, must have questioned him about her money.

'I'm sorry if this is bringing back painful memories, Mark. I ... I'm curious, that's all.'

Mark ran a hand through his hair, sighed heavily, and then picked up his wine and drank a huge mouthful. 'Yes, it is bringing back painful memories. And guilt. Maybe I should have looked harder, asked more questions, gone to Oregon myself. I always thought she'd come back when she came to her senses, you know?'

Taylor didn't know. She didn't know the woman, didn't know anything about cults, didn't have any experience with missing persons.

But she did know this sort of thing happened, and more often than people would like to think. 'What do you think we should do now?' she finally asked, when he stayed silent.

'Well, I suppose I should contact this Andrew. It's been over thirty years. The chances of him having the same phone number, or being at the same address, are pretty slim, but I'm sure it's worth the dime to make a call.'

They focused on their meals after that, and Taylor tried to switch to casual conversation. Mark asked about the bakery, and Taylor asked about the cruise she recalled Nick saying his parents had been on at Christmas.

When they finished eating, Mark pulled his phone from his pocket. 'How about we see what happens when I call that number.'

CHAPTER 17

Taylor retrieved the letter and read out the number for him. Mark entered it and pressed call, but as they'd both suspected, the number was not in service.

The disappointment on Mark's face didn't match the light tone when he spoke. 'I didn't expect that we'd have any luck. People move around a lot more these days than they used to.'

'We could check the online phone directory for San Diego ... see if he's listed?' Taylor said, trying to sound more hopeful than she felt. She suspected there would be a lot of Andrew Fletchers in San Diego, and there was no guarantee he'd even stayed in the area.

'I think I'll contact my lawyer. See what he thinks we should do. Would you mind giving me the letter? I'm pretty sure this Eve would have to be my sister, but I'm not certain it's going to prove anything.'

The possessiveness Taylor had felt earlier grabbed her again. For whatever reason, she didn't want to let go of the letter or the other contents of the box. Her mind raced, looking for a solution. 'Why don't you take a photo of the letter? That way, you can email it to your lawyer when you discuss your next steps?'

Mark nodded, his face puckering up in a thoughtful expression. 'Okay, you hang onto the original. I don't think it's going to be of any real help anyway, but don't lose it, just in case we need it for something.'

Taylor smiled. 'Thank you—I'll take good care of it. You know, it might not achieve anything, but I'm thinking I might take a drive down to Modesto. The key in this box might be for the post office box the letter was addressed to. I know it's a longshot, but you won't mind me doing that, will you?'

'Please yourself,' Mark said, not exactly dismissively, but not with much hope either.

They finished their coffees and Mark paid the bill. He wouldn't hear of Taylor splitting it with him. 'Do let me know if you have any luck with the post office box.'

~~*~~

After they'd left the hotel and said their goodbyes out on the street, Taylor decided to quickly check in at the bakery.

'Hey, Jeff, are you still on track to finish early next week?' she called out as she made her way to the back of the shop. She'd purposely walked right past the small office where Grant continued with his painting. She hadn't made up her mind about accepting his dinner invitation, and certainly didn't want to talk to him about it in front of Jeff.

'I think so. Now, just to be clear, this wall is where all your ovens are going, correct? And refrigerators along this wall?'

'That's right. And in the middle, I'll have some large work tables. They'll need power to them as well.'

'Not a problem. We can do the same thing we did in your office and bring the power up from underneath if you like?'

'I'm not sure, Jeff. I'm considering putting in some new floors back here, and I'm not sure whether I want the power coming up through them—the fewer obstacles to mop around the better, in terms of keeping the area hygienic. I'm going to look for someone to give me some advice on new flooring products.'

'Yeah, okay, we can always bring it down from the ceiling—Denver can box up some conduits and we can create a sort of power wall at each of the work benches, if that's what you'd prefer.'

She hadn't heard him approach, but suddenly Grant's voice came from right behind her.

'I told her she'd be crazy to replace these floors. They've got so much character. You'd agree, wouldn't you, Jeff?' Grant's voice sounded adversarial—like he was challenging Jeff to disagree with him.

'The floors?' Jeff said, looking down and scuffing a foot along the dirty board. 'Yeah, not my field of expertise so I really couldn't comment.'

'I'm not asking for an expert opinion, I'm just saying they have a lot of character. This place is probably well over a hundred years old. It'd be a shame to modernize it, that's all. But I do like your idea of bringing the power down to the workbenches rather than drilling up through the floor.'

The look on Jeff's face mirrored Taylor's own reaction. What the ...? Why was he so obsessed with the floors? Taylor bit back her remarks, however, not wanting to discuss it right now. She'd talk to a flooring expert and take his, or her, advice. 'Well, I only wanted to drop in and say hello since I was in town. I'll let you both get back to work.'

She turned, heading for the door, when Grant cut her off. 'You haven't forgotten about my dinner invitation, have you?' he asked.

Suddenly feeling lightheaded, she wondered if it was wise to have had the second cup of coffee. Too much caffeine sometimes did make her a bit jumpy. She ran a hand through her hair, looking down at the floor, while she considered how to answer him. 'No, of course I haven't. Sorry, I ... I'm just waiting to hear back from Alex—my sister. We made tentative plans for the weekend, but I need to hear back before I know for sure. Can I let you know tomorrow?' She felt uncomfortable with the lie, but he'd forced her to answer when she wasn't ready.

'Sure,' he said, cocking his head confidently.

One side of her did want to say yes—to put this chemistry of theirs to the test—but she still had doubts as to how smart that would be. 'Thanks, Grant. I'll probably come by tomorrow sometime, so I'll let you know then.'

She smiled, waved goodbye and dashed out to her car.

Once out of his presence, her mind cleared and her focus shifted back to the post office box. Pulling out her phone, she checked the maps to see the best route to Modesto.

It took less time to get there than she'd thought, and found the post office easily. She parked nearby and walked the short distance with trepidation. Stopping in front of a large bank of post office boxes, she took a deep breath. She knew it was too much to ask that the key would still work, but she had to try.

She scanned the numbers until she located the right one, then she held her breath as she put the key in the small lock and tried it. To her amazement, it turned.

The box was filled with what appeared to mostly be Christmas cards. As she pulled them out her heart skipped a beat. Each envelope was addressed exactly as the letter she'd found in the trinket box. She gathered them up, re-locked the box, and made her way back to her car as calmly as possible.

In the safety of her car, she organised the envelopes in date order, and opened the earliest—a letter almost identical to the one she'd previously found. Andrew, professing his love for Eve, was telling her that he'd settled in at his sister's home in San Diego. He repeated his plea for her to come to him, but also said he would understand if she didn't. He begged her to at least contact him and let him hear her voice.

Given that the letter was followed by so many cards for several years thereafter, it was nearly impossible for Taylor to believe Eve could have run off to be with Andrew. A flood of emotions washed over her—sorrow at the loss of what must have been a great love, fear for what had really happened to Eve, and a burning desire to learn the truth.

She opened the rest of the envelopes. She'd been right—they were mostly Christmas cards saying little more than an update on his family, and wishing her a safe and Merry Christmas.

The last piece of correspondence was another letter—postmarked in 1997.

Dear Eve,

Although many years have passed since we were last together, I assure you, rarely a day goes by where I don't think of you. I dream that one day we will meet again, and I know when we do it will be as if no more than a few days have passed. I continue to hold out hope that when the time is right you will reach out to me. Please believe me when I say it is not too late, it will never be too late.

My sister's ex-husband has recently remarried and he no longer objects to me relocating his daughters. I'm moving them to Chicago to stay with my brother and his family.

As for me, I have accepted a job which requires significant travel, but I'll be using my brother's home as a base. He will always know how to contact me, so I have given you his home number as well as my cell phone number. If you ever decide the time is right to track me down, I assure you, you will find me waiting for you with open arms.

With all my love,

Andrew

CHAPTER 18

'Should I ring him?' Taylor asked as soon as she finished reading the last letter to Casey.

'Oh my God, Taylor. Yes! Ring him. This is like the letters I found from Daisy to her sister, only this time the people are still alive so you can actually track them down for some answers.'

Taylor didn't want to get her hopes up—not when Mark had searched for his sister through the lawyers and come up with nothing. 'I don't know. Even this last letter was written over twenty years ago. Surely, it'll be a dead end again. He might not even be alive. Why else would he suddenly stop sending her letters and cards?'

'Who knows? There could be any number of reasons. Just ring. What have you got to lose? Worst case scenario, the number has been disconnected. Best case, he picks up the phone himself. And then there's everything in between.'

'What's the time difference from here to Chicago? It feels kinda late to be calling someone I don't know. They might even think it's a prank call.'

'Ring his number first, you silly goose. You might not even need to ring his brother in Chicago. But if you do, it's not that late—maybe two or three hours later than here, but given it's summer, it won't even be dark. Call him. You'll never be able to sleep tonight if you don't. Make the call, and then ring me back. I won't be able to sleep either if I don't know what happened.'

Taylor hung up and sat looking at the letter nervously. *What did she have to lose*? Nothing.

She quickly rang Mark to tell him about the numbers, and he was happy for her to ring, but made it clear he didn't hold much hope for success.

She dialled Andrew's cell phone first, expecting to find it no longer in service. Instead, she got a message saying she'd reached the voicemail of someone called Tom Jenkins. Andrew had probably changed jobs again.

She took a few deep breaths, entered the other number in her phone, and pressed call before she could over think it.

'Hello?' The man who answered had a deep, but not unwelcoming, voice.

'Hello,' Taylor replied, then panicked, not knowing what to say next. When her brain kicked in, she asked, breathlessly, 'May I please speak to Andrew Fletcher?'

There was a pause. That had to be a good sign. If it was a wrong number, surely he'd just say so.

'I'm David Fletcher. Andrew is my brother. Can I help you with something?'

The man's voice held curiosity, laced with something else. Perhaps suspicion? Of course he'd think it odd, getting a call from a woman he didn't know at this time of night. After all, she could be anyone, and have any number of ulterior motives for the call.

She softened her voice, trying to sound as calm and rational as possible. 'Yes, or at least I hope so. My name is Taylor Mason. I recently bought a shop which I'm renovating, and I found this letter written by Andrew to a woman named Eve. I'd like to talk to him about it, if possible.'

'Eve, did you say? This call is concerning Eve?' The suspicion had gone, replaced with a tone suggesting he thought it ludicrous that she had asked about Eve.

'Yes. I'm trying to track her down, and this letter is the most recent thing I've got in relation to her.'

'Right. And *when* did you say this letter was written?'

'Nineteen ninety-seven?' she said, knowing how desperate this had to sound.

Another long pause followed, and she began to think he might be about to hang up on her, but then he finally responded. 'Andrew travels a lot and only stays here when he's in Chicago. When he left here, he was on his way to Los Angeles. I'm not sure where he is, but I'm fairly certain he won't know anything about Eve's current whereabouts. Here's his cell phone number. Give him a call. I'm sure he'll be happy to talk to you and anxious to hear anything you might be able to tell him.'

When she hung up the call, her hands were shaking. She was so close now to finding out the truth—all she had to do was make one more call.

She entered the number into her phone and then held her breath while it rang.

After several rings, a man answered. 'Hello. This is Andrew Fletcher,' he said, in an extremely businesslike voice, not dissimilar to his brother's.

'Mr Fletcher, hello. My name is Taylor Mason,' she said, trying not to sound over excited.

'Ms Mason, what can I do for you?' he asked, his voice coming across as if concerned she was going to try to sell him something.

'Um ... I uh ... I'm calling about Eve.' She regretted the hesitancy in her voice. It wasn't how she'd wanted to come across.

The sound of a deep breath being drawn in was unmistakable.

'Mr Fletcher? Andrew? I was hoping to ask you a few questions.' She let her voice trail off softly, trying not to sound pushy.

'You're calling about Eve, and you think *I* might be able to help *you*? You're kidding, right? You don't know how long I've been waiting to hear something, anything, from or about her. I haven't seen her for ... it's been over thirty years. Are you a relative of hers?'

Taylor explained about finding the box in the butcher shop and about how it led her to finding the post office box.

'I take it she's not living in that town anymore. And if the letters were unopened, she mustn't have even seen them,' he said, his voice trailing off, his sorrow unmistakable. 'I gave up eventually ... you'll have seen how many times I wrote, but after a while ... well, I figured if she wanted to see me, she would know how to find me.'

Taylor's heart ached for this man who'd been waiting to hear from Eve for so many years. 'I'm sorry. I don't know what I hoped you could tell me. It's just ... her family—'

'You've been in contact with her family?' he asked, cutting Taylor off.

'Yes, my sister is dating Eve's nephew. His father, Mark, is Eve's brother. I met with Mark earlier today, and he believes Eve ran off to be with a cult in Oregon. Does that make any sense to you? Did she ever mention anything about it?'

His breathing grew heavier and louder. 'So, her own brother doesn't even know her whereabouts?'

'No, she never contacted him. She disappeared one day and hasn't been heard from since.'

'And her brother thought she ran off with a cult? Why on earth would he think that?'

Taylor wracked her brain, trying to recall exactly what Mark had said. 'I think it's what her husband had told him, and Mark had no reason to doubt his story because he remembered Eve talking about this cult when she was at university, as well as later when she was working in the city. He said he remembered her saying something about being envious of their freedom.'

Andrew laughed. Not a *funny-ha-ha* laugh, more of a *you've-got-to-be-kidding* kind of laugh. 'Eve? He thinks she ran off with a cult? Seriously? Look, there's no question that they were around in the eighties—I used to see them in the city too, we called them the Orange People—but Eve definitely wasn't gullible. She wouldn't have fallen for their propaganda.'

'You're certain of that? You're certain she wouldn't have run off to be with them?'

'As certain as I am that I wouldn't have. I can't believe her own brother would have thought she would.'

'Like I said, it was her husband who had suggested it, and according to Mark, her husband was heartbroken. He stayed in town for a year or so—I guess they were all hoping she'd come home—and then he moved to be near his family. Mark never heard from her husband again, but he still figured she'd just walk into town one day acting as though nothing had ever happened.'

'Her husband suggested it, you say? And her brother believed him? And never suspected foul-play? Never went looking for her?' He rattled off the questions quickly, his tone incredulous.

'Yeah, he believed him,' Taylor said, then heard a rush of breath over the phone. It was obvious that Andrew suspected the husband of something. The realisation made doubt twist in her gut. 'And as for looking for her, no, he didn't *physically* look for her, but he had lawyers search for her at one stage because she's a major beneficiary in their father's will. Even the lawyers couldn't track her down.'

Another loud intake of breath told her Andrew wasn't buying it. 'As you will have gathered from the letters, she was disloyal to her husband. Maybe he found out. Maybe he made her disappear. Did anyone question the husband?'

'I'm sure they would have. I mean, surely when he listed her as a missing person, the police would have done at least a basic investigation, right? And that would have included questioning the family?'

This time Andrew huffed out a breath dramatically. 'Maybe. Small town ... everyone knows and likes everyone. No one suggests there was any sort of foul-play. Who knows what they'd have done in terms of an investigation.'

'And you're certain this theory about her running off to a cult makes no sense?'

There was another pause and Taylor could only assume he was thinking. 'Look, Eve and I ... our connection was ...' he sighed, his pain palpable even over the phone. 'It wasn't like anything I'd ever felt before, or since. She was clever and funny and had a wonderful future to look forward to. She had choices ... she could have come with me if she'd wanted to get away from the small town. I can't even begin to imagine she would have run off to a cult as an escape.'

Taylor swallowed back her emotions, her intuition telling her he was speaking the truth and that his pain was genuine. 'I wish I could have met her ... she sounds like a wonderful person. I'm going to speak to the police and show them what I've found. They will most likely want to speak to you. May I give them your number?' As soon as she asked, she realised how stupid it was. Of course she'd give them his number, whether he was okay with it or not.

'By all means. I want to understand what happened as much as you do—probably even more.'

CHAPTER 19

After a call to both Mark and Casey to update them on her conversation with Andrew, Taylor started the car and headed home. Her heart ached for the man who had waited over thirty years to hear from Eve, only to find that to this day, no one, not even her brother, knew her whereabouts.

Mark had reiterated his intentions to speak to his lawyers, and Casey had said she'd update Nick, but neither felt there was much point in contacting the police at this late stage. This didn't sit well with Taylor, however, so she continued to ponder it as she made the hour long drive back to Masons Flat. By the time she took the turnoff into town, she'd made up her mind to speak to Denver and get his view.

Luck was on her side as she turned into Main Street and spotted Denver's truck parked outside the saloon. She pulled over and sat in her car for a moment, wanting to see Denver but not wanting to take the chance of running into Grant as she still hadn't decided whether to accept his dinner offer.

So instead of charging into the saloon, she rang him.

'Hey, Taylor, I was going to give you a call later. Jeff mentioned you guys spoke about boxing up some conduits and running power down to your workbenches rather than bringing it up from under the floor. So, I'm visualising some decorative pillars. Is that what you want?'

'To be honest, I'm not certain what I want. I need some advice on the best flooring though. I want something that's both durable and easy to keep super clean—and depending on what they recommend, I might not want to bring power up through it.'

'Ah, I see where you're coming from. You don't like the old wooden floorboards?'

'Oh, I love them for the retail area, as well as the office, but I'm pretty sure they wouldn't pass muster in the cooking area—you know, from a hygiene perspective. Do you know somewhere I can go look at flooring samples? Or do you know someone who can come out and make some recommendations?'

'Sure, I know just the guy you should talk to. I'll see if I can get him to come out tomorrow sometime. Where are you, anyway? Have you eaten? Do you want to grab a bite?'

'I'm in town, and no, I haven't eaten but I'm not hungry enough to call this my shout—I'll still owe you a nice dinner.'

Denver's soothing laugh was precisely what she needed to hear, taking away all her raw edges created by dwelling on Andrew and Eve all afternoon. 'Not a problem. I'll still let you take me somewhere a bit more upmarket, but we could pop into the steak house tonight. It's across the street from the café. They do burgers and salads and stuff too, if you don't want one of their humungous steaks.'

'Sounds perfect. Shall I meet you there in ... what, say ten minutes?'

'Sure. I'll finish my beer and head over.'

She moved her car to the other end of the street, closer to the steak house. When she saw Denver come out of the saloon, she got out and met him at the door.

'Boy, you sure look nice today. I mean, you always look nice, but you look especially nice today,' Denver said as he approached. He'd showered and put on clean clothes himself, making her wonder if he'd hoped they might end up having dinner.

'Thanks, Den. I had lunch with your uncle, so I thought I'd better look a bit smarter than I do when I'm cleaning windows,' she replied with a wink.

'Uncle Mark? Why on earth did you have lunch with him?'

'Can we get seated, and I'll fill you in on what's been happening?' she asked, linking her right arm through his and gently leading him inside.

Once seated, she gave him a full rundown of the events that led to her meeting with Mark. Denver had a serious look on his face the whole time, but he listened without interrupting.

'And now I want your opinion. Mark and Casey both think it's far too late to bring the police in. They also both feel it's entirely possible, and even likely, she did run off to be with this cult. But that doesn't make sense to me, especially after talking to Andrew.'

Taylor watched anxiously as Denver rubbed his jaw, her eyes drawn to his strong hands. Tanned and calloused from working outdoors, he was every bit the rustic cowboy. If Mark had insisted on taking the metal box to his lawyers, she wouldn't have gone to Modesto but would, instead, have driven over to see Alex. She might well have seen Denver ride. She would do that one day, soon, but for now, she desperately wanted his view. And even more desperately, she wanted him to agree with her about contacting the police.

Relief washed over her when he looked up at her and smiled. 'I think you're right—the authorities might be interested in this. I went to school with a guy who works in the Sheriff's Office, so I'm thinking we should discuss it with him and get his opinion.'

Taylor let out a long sigh. 'Fantastic. I really didn't know where to start, and given she's Mark's sister, I wasn't sure if I should go against his wishes ...'

'Yeah, look, we'll do this unofficially. I'll ring Clay, and organise a time to catch up with him over a beer. We can bring it up casually and see if he wants more information. How about we plan to have dinner in Sonora on Friday night, your shout as you like to say? We can meet him for a drink beforehand, and if he's keen to pursue this, we'll take things from there.'

'That'd be awesome—if it's not too much trouble? Is this a friend you see from time to time?'

'We bump into each other occasionally, but the last time I saw him was when he came to my thirtieth birthday. He's married with a couple of kids so he isn't going out all that often these days and, luckily, I haven't had the need to have much interaction with law enforcement.'

When the waitress arrived and read out the specials, they ordered. Afterwards, the conversation switched to the bakery.

'So, back to the advice you're after on flooring, let me give this guy I know a call and see if he's free to meet you tomorrow,' Denver said, pulling out his phone.

He made the call while Taylor excused herself to find the ladies room to wash her hands. When she returned, Denver was off the phone.

'Dave said he'd be happy to come out to see your shop, but he thinks it might be best if you meet him at his showroom first so you can see examples of the products. It's not far—just the other side of Sonora. He's got samples of a lot of new products he thinks could work. Once you've had a look at a few, he's happy to come out and give you a quote and some specific advice.'

'That sounds perfect. I don't have any plans for tomorrow, so I'll run over there and have a look.'

'And I also rang Clay. He's off work this week—doing some stuff around his house—but he's happy to come around for a cup of coffee tomorrow morning if you want to do it that way. Says he wants a couple of things from the hardware store and figures I might be able to get him a good discount,' Denver said with a wink.

'Well, if the owner can't get him a discount, no one can. What time did you want to meet?'

'Nine-thirty, at the café, if that works for you.'

Their meals arrived shortly after, and the conversation turned to the horses Denver and Travis were currently working. It was still light when they finished eating and made their way outside.

'Care to take a casual stroll before we part company?' Denver asked, hopefully.

'Sure. That would be nice,' she replied, looping her arm through his as they turned to walk along the wooden sidewalk.

'Are you starting to feel like a local yet?' Denver asked with a hint of laughter in his voice.

'Ask me again in about twenty years, maybe,' she replied in a similar tone.

He nodded slowly. 'Yeah, twenty years might make you a local. There's a few of us old dinosaurs around—ones that grew up here, like me and Travis—but these days, it seems most people have somewhere else they'd rather be. Of course, if you end up marrying into the town, the way Alex will when she and Travis finally tie the knot, that'll make you an honorary local a lot sooner.'

When he cocked his head, giving her a slight grin, she wasn't sure what to make of the statement.

'So, marrying a local makes you a local a lot quicker than becoming a business owner? That hardly seems fair,' she said, hoping her tone sounded playful.

'What can I say? It's just the way it is,' he said, his grin widening.

They strolled along to the end of the row of shops, past the front of the hotel, then crossed and peeked through the locked door into the bakery. There were ladders propped up against the wall where Jeff had been doing the electrical work in the ceiling, and a few buckets of paint up against the back wall, but other than that it was empty.

'I can't wait to open. I've been an employee my whole life, so every bit of effort I put in was for someone else's benefit. Now, it'll be for my own.'

They made their way past the saloon and continued down the street toward the café. When she glanced over at him, Denver's face had softened, and he looked deep in thought.

'It's a great feeling ... being your own boss. Of course, Travis likes to think he's my boss, given he's older and it was his idea to start breeding the Quarter Horses, but we're fifty-fifty partners in everything. We inherited the place from our parents and used some of the money to buy new stock and get started. If we're a success, or a failure, it's all on us.'

She completely understood what he was saying, and had every intention of ensuring the bakery was a great success. Why wouldn't it be, if she could develop a following of even half of what she had in Melbourne? And if Darleen would offer some product at the saloon, and the café would buy her bread and desserts, it would go a long way to her making a profit. In time, even the steak house might prefer to offer locally baked desserts and bread rolls.

When she sighed, Denver squeezed her arm. 'Hey, I hope you didn't think I was implying your bakery could be a failure. That's not what I meant.'

She shook her head. 'No, not at all; I was actually making a mental list of all the places I'll need to speak to about using my products. I'll probably provide free samples at first, and if their customers complain, they'll no doubt let me know, but if their customers are happy I see no reason why they wouldn't want to buy from me.'

He squeezed her arm against his side, and reached up with his right hand and touched her cheek, then gently traced his fingers down the line of her jaw. 'Something tells me you're going to be a great success, Taylor Mason.'

When they reached her car, he released her arm and turned to face her. She pulled out her keys and unlocked the doors, and when she looked at him again his eyes had darkened. He reached up and once again traced his fingers down the side of her face, then placed his fingers under her chin, lifting it slightly as he placed a gentle kiss on her lips.

'Thanks for having dinner with me tonight,' he said, his eyes dark with passion.

'Thank you ... for suggesting it,' she said, taking a small step back. She hadn't meant to pull away from him so much as she just wasn't entirely sure she wanted more than a friendly kiss right now, especially here, in the middle of town, where anyone could be watching. 'I ... I'm so glad you agreed with me about Eve's disappearance ... and about talking to the police about it.'

He sighed, nodding almost imperceptibly as he turned his attention down the street for a moment. When he looked at her again, his face had changed—all traces of the emotions she'd thought she'd seen having disappeared.

'Yeah, okay, I'll see you back here tomorrow, nine-thirty, for coffee with Clay. Drive safely,' he said as he opened the car door for her, and then shut it behind her once she sat.

She rolled down the window as she started the car. 'Thanks, Denver. For everything,' she said, giving him a heartfelt smile. He was one of the nicest men she'd ever met, and however things turned out between them, she hoped she could always call him a friend.

CHAPTER 20

Taylor pulled up in front of the café a few minutes before nine-thirty. When she walked in, Denver sat at a small table with a clean-cut man who appeared to be in his early thirties. Though he was dressed in casual clothes, his aura shouted "cop" even from a distance.

Denver waved her over, and both men stood.

'Clay Atkins, this is Taylor Mason. She's the great-niece of Old Man Mason; you remember him, the guy who ran the saloon and had that horse property over by Blue Gum Park?'

Clay nodded. 'Yes, of course, I remember him. Nice to meet you, Taylor.'

She smiled warmly, putting out her hand to grasp his extended one.

'Clay's on vacation this week, but normally he's one of the finest members of our Sheriff's Office,' Denver said.

'I may be on vacation this week, but I'm always working,' Clay said, releasing her hand and pulling out a chair for her.

Taylor took the seat. 'I hope once my bakery is open, you'll pop in for a taste test from time to time.'

'Bakery? Awesome. But you do know the rumour about cops and their donuts isn't quite true? I'm a croissant man, myself,' he said with a cheeky grin.

'Well then, you'll have to try mine. My croissants are scrumptious.'

Denver went to the counter to collect their coffees while Taylor began to run through the events of the past few days, starting with the discovery of the metal box and ending with her call to Andrew Fletcher. Clay listened with great interest, never interrupting, just nodding encouragingly and with the occasional umm or uh-huh thrown in. When she finished talking, he continued to nod as a frown deepened across his brow.

Denver, who'd appeared anxious since he'd returned with the coffees but had shown great restraint in not interrupting, finally spoke. 'I think this guy she was having an affair with is hiding something. I mean, who would keep paying for a post office box for all those years on the off chance a woman he'd had sex with a few times might check it one day? It sounds fishy to me ... and more like it was done to throw anyone looking for her off the scent.'

Clay looked at Denver, cocking his head with a gentle shrug, clearly still deep in thought. He picked up his coffee and took a long sip before finally saying something. 'That's definitely one possibility. However, if Mrs Harrison had run off to be with him, it seems strange she'd have left that box where it could be so easily found, don't you think?'

Denver shrugged. 'Yeah, well, maybe she forgot about it? Maybe she remembered later, and so he wrote those letters so it didn't look like she'd run off to be with him.'

Clay nodded his head, his mouth pursing.

Taylor sighed. 'It's usually the spouse, isn't it, in cases like this? She could be dead ... her husband could have found out about Andrew, and killed her and buried her ... anywhere.'

Clay turned to her, raising a brow. 'And that's another possibility.'

When Taylor caught Denver's eye, he looked as confused as she was. Neither spoke, waiting for Clay to say something else.

'And it's always possible her brother was correct. Mrs Harrison could well have run off to be with that cult in Oregon, taking only a few personal items and whatever money she could get her hands on,' he said. 'There have been many cults over the years which have attracted Americans into their midst, Taylor—you've just got to look at Waco, Texas, and Charles Manson, and of course there was Jonestown. And in the 1980s, there were the Orange People, congregating in Oregon. It's entirely possible she went to them for reasons we may never know.'

Taylor didn't want it to be that simple. She didn't know much about Eve, but even so, she couldn't see her joining a cult. Andrew had said it wasn't in her character, and she wanted to believe him rather than Mark.

Clay took a sip of his coffee and then set it down. 'How about I see if I can find a file of what was done back in 1985. I might also see if there's anything on the husband. Don Harrison, you said, right? And he moved to Arizona?'

'Yes, according to Eve's brother, Mark Gold, he moved there about a year later ... so sometime in 1986.'

'Okay, leave it with me for a few days. I'm not suggesting we open an official investigation at this stage, but I can make a few calls and do a little poking around.'

'Do you want the box and the letters? I have everything in my car.'

Clay rubbed his hand across his jaw, his expression thoughtful. 'Not at this stage. You hang onto them, but if we turn this into something a bit more official, I'll need them.'

When it became obvious the conversation about Eve had come to an end, Denver turned to Clay. 'Did you want to head over to the hardware store now?'

Clay smiled. 'Nah, I was just kidding. I don't need anything at the moment.'

After Clay said goodbye, Taylor and Denver continued to stand outside the café. 'Do you want to walk down to the bakery with me and see how the work is going?' Denver asked.

Taylor reached up and ran her hand through her hair, shoving a wayward lock behind her ear, noticing how Denver watched her every movement. She spoke without thinking, letting the moment guide her. 'Grant's asked me out to dinner.'

Denver stood taller, taking a small step back from her. He bit his lower lip as he looked down the street toward the bakery. He spoke without looking at her. 'Has he?'

She nodded, chewing on her bottom lip. 'I haven't said I'd go yet. I ... I told him I had to check with my sister ... that we had tentative plans. It wasn't true; I just wanted time to think about it.'

Denver still didn't look at her. 'And you're asking my opinion? Is that why you've mentioned it?'

'I don't know ... maybe? I mean, would it bother you if I went to dinner with him?'

She couldn't see much of his face as he stared off into the distance, but from what she could see, it appeared Denver was weighing up the question. She wasn't sure how she'd summoned the courage to raise it with him, and now she wasn't sure she should have. And the longer he remained silent, the more certain she became that it had been a very bad idea.

'If you want to go, you should. He seems a nice enough guy. And it's not like we've made any sort of commitment or anything.'

His tone said what his words hadn't. He was upset, and she wasn't sure how to take that. Did he care for her more than she'd guessed? She felt sick at the thought of hurting him.

'No, look, it doesn't feel right. I think that's why I've hesitated. I've never dated two men at a time. And we are—sort of—dating, aren't we?'

Now he turned to look at her, and she could see the hurt in his eyes. 'I thought we were. I thought we were just taking things slowly, but if you want to go out to dinner with Grant, I think you should.'

She reached out and put her hand on his forearm. 'I'm not certain I do want to, it's just ... I'm not certain I don't, either. I'm not sure what I think.'

The muscles on the side of his face tightened. 'I think you should go,' he eventually said.

He started to walk off, but Taylor squeezed his arm. 'Please don't be angry; let's not let this be a problem between us, okay?'

'Oh, I'm not angry, Taylor. I'm ... disappointed, I suppose.'

She put on her warmest smile, still holding onto his arm. 'I'll suggest we have dinner here in town ... at the steak house ... tomorrow night. It won't be like a real date.'

Denver smiled, and shrugged, his look suggesting he'd become resigned to her going out with Grant. 'You don't have to do that ... treat it like it's not a real date, I mean. Go out with him. See how you feel about it. And if he's not up to scratch, you know I'll be here waiting to see you again. In fact, why don't we plan to go out on Saturday night?'

She couldn't believe how well Denver was taking this, and suspected if the situation were reversed, she'd struggle to behave so maturely. She liked him so much, and couldn't quite understand why she even felt obliged to go out with Grant other than the fact she got tingles through her whole body every time she stood anywhere near him.

'If you're sure you're okay about it, I'll say yes ... to both.'

Denver sighed, a look of relief washing over him. Then he smiled. 'I'll make a reservation at an Italian restaurant in Sonora. We can go dancing afterwards.'

'I'd like that,' she said, truly meaning it.

'Great. So ... did you want to head to the bakery with me now?'

She hesitated. It was one thing to have told Denver about the date with Grant, it was a totally different thing to accept Grant's offer in front of him. 'No, I'll let you go speak to them. I might call past later. I'm going over to see Dave about the flooring, remember?'

'Right. He'll look after you. Drive safely,' he said, leaning forward and kissing her cheek. When he stepped back, he stared into her eyes for a moment. 'You mean a lot to me, Taylor. I may not always show it, but you do. Enjoy your dinner with Grant, but not too much, okay?'

Heat rushed through her, and she suddenly could think of nothing worse than having dinner with Grant. But she'd go, now that she'd told Denver about it. She'd go, and then it would be behind her, and she could focus her attention on getting the bakery open and continue to see how things went with Denver. 'Okay,' she answered, her voice catching. 'I won't.'

When Denver headed down the street, she got in her car, pulled out her phone and got the directions to the shop in Sonora. Maybe looking at floors was exactly what she needed.

CHAPTER 21

Armed with a few samples of the flooring options Dave had recommended, Taylor called into the bakery just after lunch. The door was shut, but not locked, even though no one was around.

She headed to the office, pleased to find the extent of progress Grant had made. The walls were completed, and the soft yellow paint had come up even better than she'd hoped. She pulled out the floor samples and held them up to the wall—there were two which looked awesome so it would most likely come down to availability.

She turned toward the highlight window and sighed. Now, as it neared completion, she could envision herself here, in this office, sitting at her desk with the hint of natural light coming from behind her.

The sound of footsteps and male voices alerted her to the return of Jeff and Grant. She walked to the front of the shop and said hello.

'The office is looking fabulous, Grant, thank you. So ... you've started out here now, I suppose?'

Grant beamed at her praise then nodded toward the east facing window. 'I've started over there, and I'll work my way around. The walls in here have a few holes to be filled, where it seems there was shelving, but they aren't too bad.'

'Great. And how are you going, Jeff? Any hiccups?'

'None what-so-ever. Have you thought any more about the floors? About whether you want me to bring the wiring up from underneath or drag it down through the ceiling?'

'No, I haven't decided. Is it holding you up?'

'Not really; I have enough other stuff to keep me busy for a few days.'

'Good. I've got some samples here of the flooring materials I'm thinking about. Dave is going to come out and give me a quote, and we'll see what he says about whether the wiring can come up through the floors or whether it's better to bring it down through pillars.'

Grant looked particularly interested. 'Well, I'll say it again ... I'd be doing everything possible to keep the floors intact in case someone wants to strip off the top layer of flooring later and go back to the floorboards. With that in mind, I'd be inclined to bring it down through those pillars.'

She turned to Grant, cocking her head as she thought about what he'd suggested. He could be right, to keep flexibility for the future. But she had no idea what Dave would recommend and thought it even possible he'd say they had to rip up all the current flooring.

She chose not to acknowledge Grant's comments. 'I'll let you both get back to work then. I just wanted to see how these colours looked up against the paint,' she said, making her way toward the door.

Jeff headed to the back area, but Grant followed her. 'So, are we having dinner this weekend?'

'Oh, yes. I'm free tomorrow night as it turns out. I thought we might go to the steak house here in town if that's okay with you?'

The smile erupting on his face made him look younger. She'd never asked his age, but had assumed he was roughly the same as her. Now that she thought about it, he did look like he could be several years younger. Not that it mattered. They were having dinner, not raising a family.

'Perfect. Shall I come get you ... around seven?' he asked, now standing so close she could feel his breath on her face.

A tingle of anticipation rushed through her, but she tried to ignore it. 'How about I meet you there? Save you coming out and then back in again.' She didn't know where he lived, but she had seen him drive out of town in the opposite direction once.

'Seven it is. I'm looking forward to getting to know you better, Taylor,' he said, not taking his eyes off her.

She could no longer ignore it—that feeling rushing through her, making her so much more aware of his maleness than she'd ever been with any other man. What was it about him? Did Casey feel this way about every man she dated? Casey always raved about chemistry, but before meeting Grant, Taylor hadn't experienced what she'd been referring to. For her, relationships were always based on mutual interests and personality. But if this was what chemistry felt like, no wonder Casey had always been so addicted to it.

~~*~~

Taylor showered, washed her hair, and got ready to go. She'd chosen a dress with a green background that brought out the colour of her eyes. Although not wanting to appear to be trying too hard, she did want to make some effort.

They met outside the restaurant at seven. Grant looked as though he'd just come from the shower, smelling of some alluring aftershave. His blue eyes fairly twinkled when he spotted her.

'Wow, you look fantastic,' Grant said as he walked up. Putting one hand on her lower back he leaned in and kissed her cheek.

'Thank you. You scrub up pretty well yourself,' she said, taking in the pale blue shirt that matched his eyes, and his strong arms below his partially rolled-up sleeves. He was all tanned muscle, and the epitome of what she'd always thought of as a real man.

The waitress seated them, and Grant immediately ordered some pre-dinner drinks. He had bourbon on the rocks, while she chose a gin and tonic. When the waitress brought their drinks, she also brought what she referred to as breadsticks and a small dish of artichoke dip—on the house. Taylor was impressed with the food, even if the dipping sticks were nowhere near as good as her own grissini.

After a few minutes, Grant ordered himself another drink, but Taylor decided to pace herself.

Grant chatted about his youth, telling her about growing up in Arizona and spending summers in South Dakota with his grandparents. Then he asked her about what it had been like to grow up in Australia and what had made her want to move to California, in general, and this small town in particular. Taylor meant to ask him what had brought him to Masons Flat but the waitress came to take their orders just as the thought struck her.

Taylor was beginning to feel light-headed as she hadn't eaten much all day and knew she needed some real food so she ordered a chicken breast stuffed with apricots and almonds, while Grant indulged in the largest steak on the menu. He also ordered a bottle of red wine to drink with their dinner.

Even after finishing their meal, Taylor still felt slightly light-headed. She turned down his offer for an after-dinner drink, but when he offered to drive her home, she figured it was a wise choice. After all, with those muscles of his, the alcohol hardly seemed to have done more than get him talking. She, on the other hand, had either had too much to drink, or her hormones were affecting the way the alcohol hit her. Whatever it was, she accepted his offer, deciding she could walk back into town in the morning to collect her car.

When Grant pulled up in front of her house, she quickly got out of the car, but he still came around and walked her to the door. He then stood patiently while she got her keys out. When he spoke, she expected him to thank her for a lovely evening, but instead he said, 'Hey, I meant to ask ... Jeff said something about you finding a metal box under the floorboards in the office. Anything interesting in it?'

Her giggles vanished with the serious question, and her intuition warned her not to say too much. 'The box? Oh, just some trinkets, nothing interesting.'

For a brief moment, he looked disappointed. 'Maybe you could show me? I've always been interested in this sort of thing.'

She tilted her head, her brow creasing inquisitively. 'This sort of thing? What, metal boxes?'

'Yeah, sort of. More like ... hidden boxes. Maybe the trinkets are more important than you think.'

'I doubt it. My guess is it was used to store money from time to time, but if there had been money in it, it was long gone,' she said, unlocking the door and opening it. 'Anyway, thank you for a lovely evening. I really enjoyed the meal and our conversation.'

He sighed, putting on what struck her as an artificial smile for a moment. She wondered if he was trying to decide whether or not to kiss her goodnight. Finally, his smile became more genuine. 'Are you doing anything on Sunday? I found a nice walking trail not far out of town. We could go for a walk and have a picnic lunch?'

The question took her by surprise. So much so, she couldn't think of a reason to say no. 'Sure, that sounds nice,' she answered, stepping inside the house.

'Great. I'll pick you up ... say around eleven?'

He gave her a quick peck on the cheek before heading to his car. It was nice, implying more to come, but not being in a rush to get there.

As she went inside, she remembered she was going out to dinner with Denver the following night. Three dates in one weekend. What sort of woman had she become?

~~*~~

Denver arrived exactly on time, his face lighting up as she opened the door.

'Wow, you look ... incredible,' he said with a bit of a whistle. 'Nice dress.'

'Thanks, I borrowed it from Alex ... and I'm kind of amazed how well it fits,' she said as she spun around to make the skirt flare.

She'd been surprised when Alex had suggested it—surprised because she'd barely noticed how much weight she'd dropped since arriving back in California, and would never have thought anything belonging to Alex would ever fit her. Perhaps being away from the bakery—where she'd been tempted to eat so many of the unsold pastries—was good for her. She'd have to keep this in mind going forward.

Alex clearly had noticed, however, saying it would be perfect for a date with dancing. And as soon as she saw it, Taylor knew Alex was right. With its sweetheart neckline, capped sleeves, empire waist and flared skirt, it would look superb on the dance floor if she could manage a twirl. And, with its pale blue background, covered with splashes of red, white and orange flowers and emerald green leaves, the dress was perfect for her colouring.

As soon as they'd pulled out of the driveway, Denver looked across at her. 'So ... how was it?'

She tried, unsuccessfully, to hide her smile. 'How was what?' she said, trying to sound innocent.

He rolled his eyes. 'Your date.'

'Oh, that. It was fine. The food is good there, as you very well know.'

'I didn't mean the food.''

'Oh.' She knew exactly what he meant.

'So?'

She ducked her head down, and looked up at him through her lashes. 'It was ... fine. He's quite entertaining when he's had a couple of drinks. He really opened up. Told me about his youth—growing up in Arizona and spending summers in South Dakota.'

'Arizona? Huh, I could have sworn he'd told me he was from New Mexico.'

Taylor's gut twisted momentarily as she suddenly recalled that Arizona was where Eve's husband, Don, had moved. Why hadn't it struck her at the time when he said it? She brushed the sensation aside—after all, Arizona was a huge state. 'No, I'm sure he said Arizona and South Dakota. He talked about water skiing at Lake Havasu, and trips to the Grand Canyon and other national parks.'

'Yeah? Okay, it doesn't matter.'

'Come to think of it, I meant to ask him what brought him up here to Masons Flat, but then the conversation changed. Had you ever asked him?'

Denver cocked his head, thinking. 'I'm pretty sure it had something to do with a sister who lives in Twain Harte—it's not far from here.'

She was grateful as Denver focussed on his driving and the discussion about Grant ended. She looked out the window, admiring the scenery, and it wasn't long before they arrived at what appeared to be a rather upmarket restaurant.

The maître d' met them at the door and showed them to a small, private, table in the corner. White linen, crystal glasses and polished silver confirmed her first impression—Denver had chosen well, indeed.

After they ordered, Denver picked up his glass. 'A toast,' he said while she picked up her glass. 'To the start of something I hope will become very special.'

Heat rushed through her at his words. She, too, hoped their relationship was special—but exclusive dating special or best friends forever special? The question haunted her. 'Oh, yes, thank you ... cheers, Denver.'

Their glasses clinked, and she took a sip. The wine was superb, as was the meal when it arrived: delicate ravioli filled with spinach and ricotta cheese for starters, followed by chicken cacciatore done to perfection, and a delicate tiramisu for dessert. She couldn't fault anything with either the meal or the company.

Nor could she fault anything to do with the rest of the evening.

They made their way to the same bar where they'd danced to Tommy and the Tripods the weekend before, only tonight they didn't have a live band. Instead, the jukebox pumped out rockabilly songs one after another. The smaller crowd on the dance floor left plenty of room for Denver to help her. The moment he took her hand, his strength penetrated her, giving her confidence that she could do this. It wasn't long before they were swinging to the lyrics of song after song and she wasn't even tripping. She couldn't wipe the smile off her face as he swung her around and pulled her in close with his strong arms. Then, when a slow song finally came on, and the words "Hey ... hey, baby ..." echoed across the room, he pulled her in close and held her there against his chest. And right then, something clicked into place. This, surely, was where she belonged, wasn't it?

By the time Denver pulled up in front of her house and walked her to the door, it was after one. With keys in hand, she turned to him.

'Did you want to come in? For a ... coffee, or a nightcap?' The feelings she'd experienced on the dance floor still lingered, chasing away her previous uncertainties.

He bit his lower lip and blinked slowly. 'Of course I do, but ... I think you need to sort out your feelings for Grant before we get too much further down the track. I mean, if I come in, I won't be leaving in a hurry.'

Hearing Denver say Grant's name broke the spell that had captivated her all evening. Denver was right—she had to slow things down. Denver was a wonderful man, but even if he wasn't, she wasn't the sort of woman who would toy with his feelings.

'Okay,' she answered, trying to deter a frown threatening to creep onto her face.

He obviously saw it, as he reached up and smoothed her forehead, rubbing his thumb across one eyebrow, and then cupping her cheek in the palm of his hand.

'I'll be here for you, Taylor. I'll always be here for you, whatever you decide.'

He took a step closer and wrapped his arms around her, rubbing the small of her back gently. When his grip loosened, she leaned back to look up into his eyes, liking what she saw in them: warmth, honesty, patience. She'd never known such a good man. But did she deserve him? Didn't he deserve someone who knew his worth and accepted his attention without hesitation?

When a slight smile touched his eyes, she felt her own smile creep onto her face. And when he leaned down and kissed her, she responded with all her heart. And for that moment, all doubt vanished.

CHAPTER 22

Taylor woke in a state of euphoria, wondering how she could have ever questioned her feelings for Denver. Then she remembered her picnic date with Grant. He'd be picking her up at eleven. She immediately began to regret that she'd agreed to go, but she hadn't been brought up to cancel on such short notice. Instead, after a quick shower, she put on her oldest pair of jeans, a ratty tee-shirt, and tied a hoodie around her waist in an attempt to look as unappealing as possible.

When he pulled into the driveway, she dashed out, saving him from coming to her door.

'Ready for a bit of adventure?' he asked as she climbed into the passenger seat.

'Absolutely,' she replied, pointing to her hiking boots. She'd had them for years, having bought them for a climb at Hanging Rock with a group of friends several years earlier. She couldn't recall them being on her feet since that day, and had wondered why she'd even bothered to bring them with her to California, but right now, she was glad she had—especially when she looked over to see he, too, was wearing hiking boots. She wondered what his idea of a gentle hike would be like.

When they'd gone over the bridge and turned right onto the highway, Grant looked at her and smiled. 'I spotted the signs to this place as I drove home one day, so I went up to check it out. It's a fairly easy hike, with some benches and a monument at the top—one of those directional markers.'

'Oh, I like those,' she replied, the uncertainty at having accepted his invitation beginning to dissipate now that they were on their way.

The climb was, as Grant had said, fairly easy. There was one section where the rocks were slippery, but Grant went up ahead of her and reached down, offering assistance. His hand was large and calloused, and grabbing onto it made her feel safe. They climbed the rest of the way easily and soon found themselves standing at the top of the hill, in a cleared area with uninterrupted views.

'What a magnificent view,' she said, looking off into the distance. 'It wasn't a bad climb, either, other than that one spot. I'll have to bring my sisters here one day.'

'I thought you'd like it,' he said as he began pointing out landmarks.

After they'd looked all around, he led her toward a bench, opened up his small backpack, and set out lunch on the bench between them. He'd brought a stick of salami, a small loaf of sourdough bread, and a jar of mustard, along with a couple of bottles of water. Simple, but sitting in the fresh air with the views of distant hills, it was just right.

On the drive back Grant took a slightly different route. He pulled onto a dirt road, making his way along quite slowly. The homes along this road were on fairly large blocks of land and, although not new, they were not the quaint miner's cottages and renovated heritage homes she'd seen closer to town. Some were in a state of disrepair with gutters full of weeds and paint peeling off, while others looked like they'd been well looked after over the years. Personally, she could think of nowhere worse to live than on one of these old washboard dirt roads.

At one stage, she was certain she could feel Grant staring at her, but he said nothing. He continued to drive slowly, presumably so as not to stir up too much dust. Then, just before they reached the end of the road, Grant cleared his throat and spoke without turning to look at her.

'Interesting little houses, don't you think, with the porches all around the front? Guess they were built in the days when people would sit out on their porch and chat with their neighbours. Nowadays, most people don't even know their neighbours.'

She stared at his profile, thinking how insightful it was of him to make the comment. She'd only looked at the houses in terms of their current problems, not their inherent design advantages. He was right—it would have been nice to live in one of those houses when they were new. Mind you, they probably weren't close enough together to speak to your neighbours, unless they were walking past on the street.

He stopped when he reached the end of the road, then turned right onto the highway to make the short drive back to Masons Flat. When the route back to her place took him past the front of the bakery, he looked over at the building and nodded. 'It's quite a nice-looking old building you've bought. Looks like it's been as neglected over the years as some of those homes we passed on the way back to town. The building is lucky—being bought by someone with the means to fix it up. And you're lucky to be able to do it—I mean, you know, for such a young woman.'

She knew what he meant, and even considered telling him about her inheritance, but thought better of it at the last second. 'It is a lovely old building. I'm so glad there isn't anything structurally wrong with it. A bit of paint on the exterior and a new sign, and it'll look loved again, that's for sure.'

As he made the turn into Mason Street, he continued. 'You know, I still think it'd be a real shame to destroy the old floors in there. When's your guy coming out to have a look?'

She could feel the frown as it tightened her forehead. What was it with this obsession with the floors? 'Tomorrow afternoon, why?'

'Oh, I just want to hear what he's got to say.'

He pulled into her driveway and stopped the car, then turned and looked at her. She could feel that he wanted her to invite him in, and one side of her did think she should—for a coffee at least—but a sense of discomfort had been triggered by him bringing up the floorboards again. It was simply too strange that he'd keep talking about them. 'Look,' she lied, as the silence grew uncomfortable, 'I'd love to invite you in, but I'm heading over to see my sister.'

'No problem,' he said, his eyes narrowing slightly before a grin took over his face. 'I guess I'll see you at the bakery tomorrow afternoon then. Oh, and maybe you can show me where you found the metal box, if that's ok?'

'The box? I thought I did tell you? It was in the office, under a loose floorboard. You'll need to fix the boards down when you sand them ... so sure, I'll show you which ones tomorrow. Thanks again for the lovely day, and I'll see you tomorrow.'

When she jumped out of the car, he made no move to follow her. One side of her wished he had—the side wondering what a goodbye kiss from Grant would feel like—but the other side, the side leaning more and more toward Denver, was glad he hadn't.

As she watched his car disappear down the street, the thought which had been teasing at the back of her mind finally surfaced. Where had Eve and her husband lived? Had they lived in town, or had they lived along a dusty road on the other side of the highway?

Walking back to the kitchen, she decided to call Mark.

'I remember Clay,' Mark said after Taylor said he was going to do some unofficial digging around. 'He hung out with both Nick and Denver when they were kids. Clay was always a good kid—polite, respected his elders. Bet he's pretty good at his job. If Clay thinks there is merit in doing some investigating, there could well be.'

'I think it's a good idea, too. Oh ... now before I let you go, do you remember where Eve lived?'

'Where she and Don lived after they got married? Sure, it was north of the highway, on a dirt road. I can't remember the name of the street, but I can picture it with the scattered and well separated houses. I could look it up if it matters?'

CHAPTER 23

An hour later, Alex and Taylor were finishing up their discussion on the plans for the upcoming wedding. Both Alex and Travis had been married before, so they wanted to keep it simple, and were thinking of just a small gathering at the house. Alex wanted to use a marriage officiate since neither of them had any religious affiliation. Taylor agreed it sounded like a wonderful idea.

Talking about marriage made her think even more about Denver, and how odd it was that three sisters could have ended up romantically involved with the two Gold brothers and their cousin, who was also a Gold. But rather than making her feel warm and fuzzy about her growing feelings toward Denver, it made her question them even more—it was, after all, too unrealistic, wasn't it?

When they finished their coffee, Taylor stood up to leave.

Alex walked her out, and when they got to her car, she placed a hand on Taylor's forearm. 'Look, Denver and Travis are working with a couple of the horses. I don't think you've ever watched them work their horses, have you?'

'Only from a distance,' Taylor said, looking toward the arena where she could now see the men on horseback.

'Come watch for a bit. It's pretty amazing to see these horses in action. Travis says some of it is the natural talent of Quarter Horses ... a bit like Border Collies and Kelpies and how they have natural herding instincts, I guess.'

Not being any sort of farm girl, Taylor had only a vague idea what Alex was referring to, but she had seen a few minutes of some competition once, where men were whistling as a means to communicate with their dogs as they herded sheep into pens.

They made their way over to the arena and stopped at the edge to peer through the rails. Both men appeared as one with their horses, and appeared oblivious to their arrival.

The longer they watched, the clearer it became that there was something special about both these horses and their riders. The men barely moved in the saddles as their horses ducked and weaved in the enclosed arena, each one in turn chasing a cow as though playing a game of cat and mouse. She didn't once see either of the men lift their hands or give their horses any physical instructions, but she couldn't tell whether they, like the dog handlers, might have been making some soft whistling sounds as cues.

They'd stood watching for several minutes before Travis finally looked over in their direction. His cow had been coerced into a small pen, and Denver was just getting his cow into the one next to it. A moment later, the two men rode over and stopped in front of them.

'Hey, ladies. What'd you think of these two youngsters?' Travis said, patting his horse on the neck and then wiping his sweat-covered hand on his jeans.

'Impressive, that's for sure. They're beautiful animals, don't you agree, Taylor?' Alex said, turning toward Taylor.

Taylor nodded, then turned toward Denver when he spoke.

'Some of the best we've ever bred,' Denver said with pride in his voice, and then he, too, leant down and ran his hand along his horse's neck, rubbing rather than patting the way Travis had. The gesture, while no doubt done innocently enough, carried with it all sorts of suggestions in Taylor's mind.

She tried to raise her gaze to meet Denver's eyes but couldn't yet tear her eyes away from his arm, now draped across the horse's neck as he leant forward in the saddle.

There was something incredibly sexy about seeing him this way, mounted on this beautiful horse, covered in dust and sweat—his shirt sleeves rolled up, exposing the muscles in his forearms, his jeans straining across his thighs.

Finally, she managed to look up. Her eyes found his, and for a moment the strong connection made her forget where she was, and that Travis and Alex were right there with them.

'Erm,' she said, clearing her throat, 'they are gorgeous, for sure.'

The sound of a soft laugh coming from Travis broke the momentary spell, and she turned to see the cheeky look on his face.

'Clearly, we need to get you spending more time over here, Taylor. Usually girls are a lot younger than you when they develop horse fever, but from the look on your face, you've well and truly been bitten by the bug.'

Taylor could feel the heat rising in her cheeks, wondering if Travis was really so naïve as to think her staring had more to do with the horse than with his younger brother.

~~*~~

When Taylor arrived at the bakery late the following afternoon, the flooring specialist hadn't yet arrived. Denver was there, however, going through the work done so far and discussing what still had to be done. He and Grant were inspecting the floorboards in what would be her kitchen as she walked in.

'Some of these are pretty rotten,' Denver said after greeting her, pointing out the area near the sink. 'There's rot all around the base of the sink, and it looks to me that a lot of water had come in through the back door as well.'

His manner was all professionalism today and whatever spell had been cast while she'd watched him ride, seemed a distant memory.

'It's a shame, isn't it, but I suspect this sink would have been used all day every day,' she said, thinking about all the cleaning up that would be necessary in a butcher's shop.

'Ah, it's not so bad. I've done up lots of floorboards. This will be an easy fix,' Grant said, catching her eye and speaking matter-of-factly.

Denver looked at him but didn't reply. Then he turned to Taylor again. 'Maybe they were smokers, propping the back door open a lot. Since it faces north, and there's no awning over the door, these floors could have seen a lot of rain on them.'

She tilted her head. 'I rarely think about smokers anymore, but you're probably right. I suppose it's only been in the last decade or so that smoking has been banned in workplaces.'

'Come on,' Grant said, bending down and running a hand over the floors, 'it's easy to sand it back and put a coat of varnish on it. That's what I'd be doing ... if this were my place.'

Denver gave her an unmistakable *What's up with him?* look, and then continued almost as if Grant hadn't spoken. 'Let's see what Dave has to say before we get too worried about it.'

~~*~~

When Dave had finished looking at the floors and made his final recommendations for polymer flooring throughout at least the back portion of the bakery, he and Denver left together. With Jeff still working out the back, Taylor was free to speak quietly to Grant.

Alone.

Convinced he knew something about Eve—between his fixation about the floors and the metal box, to his driving slowly past the house where Eve had lived—she decided the perfect way to get him to open up about his knowledge would be over a few wines.

'I had such a lovely time the other night, and I've been thinking ... would you be free for dinner again, maybe tonight or tomorrow night? My shout, since you paid last time?'

Grant's left eyebrow rose provocatively as a slow smile touched his lips. He was clearly flattered by her offer. 'Sure, that sounds like a great idea. Here in town again, or do you want to venture to somewhere a little more interesting?'

'Oh, I'd be happy back at the steak house or the hotel, but if you want to go somewhere else, I'm fine with wherever you want to go.'

'Leave it with me,' he said, nodding. 'I'll pick you up at seven.'

~~*~~

When they arrived at the hotel, Grant was able to park right out the front. There were only two other tables with guests, and neither were anywhere near them. Taylor was pleased with the lack of other patrons, as this would give them the perfect opportunity to talk more openly.

When the waitress brought the menus, Grant ordered a bottle of wine and asked for a few minutes to decide on their food orders. A moment later, the waitress returned with the bottle and poured it for them.

'I really enjoyed our hike and picnic yesterday,' Taylor said as she picked up her glass to take in the fragrant bouquet of the deep red wine.

'So did I,' he said, flashing a quick, though somewhat artificial looking, smile.

'It was an interesting route you took on the way back to town—it felt like we'd gone back in time. What made you drive down that road?' she asked, looking at him through her lashes as she took a sip of the wine.

Grant cocked his head, looking as though trying to recall, but she was certain it was an act. His driving down there had been deliberate. After a moment, he shrugged. 'I don't remember to be honest.'

She set her glass down and skimmed the menu. After the waitress had returned and taken their orders, she tried again. 'There was something, oh I don't know, familiar perhaps, about that dirt road. I'm not sure why but I had the oddest feeling as we drove along there.'

Grant's eyes lit up. 'How so?'

Now she was stuck. 'I'm not sure ... I mean, it felt like I'd been there before, but I couldn't have been. I know I haven't since returning to the area, and when we were here over Christmas we didn't investigate the local area all that much. It was just this real odd déjà vu moment, you know?'

Grant picked up his glass, surveying the room. No further patrons had come in, but even so, when he next spoke he leaned in across the table, urging her to lean toward him as well. He then spoke, in a soft voice. 'I think I felt something too—I think that's why I took that road, because something drew me there. Are you sure you haven't been there? Sure you haven't had some reason to check out those houses?'

She shook her head, both to say no and to try to shake the foggy sensation starting to come over her. She hadn't eaten much during the day—was the half glass of wine too much for her on an empty stomach?

Over dinner, she purposely avoided talking any further about the road or the bakery and tried to get him to open up about his life, and particularly his childhood. He, however, continually diverted the conversation back to her life. At least by the time they finished eating her light-headedness had gone.

The night air was balmy, so she rolled down the window for the short trip back to her place. Grant pulled into the driveway, shut off the car, and went around and opened the passenger door for her. When she got out, he brushed up against her slightly, sending a rush of anticipation through her whole body. Why was her body defying her mind? Hadn't she made up her mind that Denver held her interest?

'Did you want to come in ... for a coffee?' she asked once she'd opened the door.

'Thought you'd never ask,' he answered.

As he followed her down the hall toward the kitchen, she became even more aware of his physical presence. Keeping up a steady pace, she didn't slow until she reached the counter top where she deposited her handbag. When she turned, he was right there, only inches from her, his tall frame towering over her and making her feel petite once again, the way he had the first time they'd met. She drew in a settling breath, but it seemed to make things worse, not better.

Swallowing hard, she forced words from her mouth. 'How do you have your coffee?'

He hesitated, weighing up his answer. 'With one teaspoon of sugar.'

Turning her back to him while she made the coffee gave her a few minutes to focus on something other than his strong biceps and shoulders, but when she turned to hand him the cup, he'd moved, now standing at the window overlooking the garden.

'Your coffee,' she said, placing both cups on the table and taking a seat.

He turned to her and began to roll up his sleeves as he walked to the table. It had been an innocent act, rolling up his sleeves, but the effect it had on her body was anything but innocent.

'Thanks,' he said, taking the seat next to her, not across from her as she'd anticipated.

He picked up his cup, blew on the steaming liquid, and then turned to her and smiled. 'Smells divine; I can rarely say no to a cup of coffee after dinner.'

He angled his chair toward her and rested his elbow on the table. When he spread his legs, his thigh touched hers, sending energy through her traitorous body.

'Coffee sometimes keeps me awake—I usually have herb tea at night, but since I was making coffee ...'

He smiled. When he cocked his head to one side and ran his tongue over his bottom lip, the energy between them ramped up a notch.

Putting his cup down on the table, he reached over and gently pushed an errant strand of hair back from the corner of her mouth. 'Your hair is so beautiful, Taylor. I'm sure every man you meet can't wait to run his hands through it.'

Tingles ran through her as an image of him, running his hands through her hair while making love to her, teased at the back of her mind. She tried to brush the thoughts away, but they persisted.

As she tried to speak, her voice caught. She tried again. 'No one's ever said anything quite that direct to me about my hair, but I have certainly had some compliments.'

'Compliments ... I bet. I haven't been able to stop thinking about it, and what it would be like to be looking up at you with your hair brushing against my face.'

Her eyes flew open wide as she struggled to draw in a breath—it was as if he'd read her mind.

She picked up her cup, desperate to break the mood developing between them. 'I forgot to put milk in mine. Be right back,' she said, heading to the fridge. She never had milk in her coffee other than in cappuccinos, but tonight she'd make an exception. As she poured the milk, the haze that had overcome her began to dissipate. She put the milk back in the fridge, but rather than returning to the table, she walked to the window.

It was still early enough in the evening that she could make out shapes in the garden, even if the colours had faded. She pretended to study a patch of dirt where a shrub had been removed by the gardener. 'I'm trying to decide what to put out the front here. A few of the plants died over summer, leaving some bare patches.'

'I'm not much of a gardener,' Grant said, coming over and standing beside her, his maleness once again so powerful she struggled not to touch him.

'No, neither am I. Casey is the gardener in the family. I might give her a call for some ideas. I probably need the sort of gardens you'd have had in Arizona. It's dry there, so you must have a lot of hardy plant varieties—ones that don't require much in the way of either water or attention?' She blew on her coffee, which clearly wasn't hot given she'd just put milk in it, then made her way back to the table, purposely taking a seat on the opposite side of the table to where Grant's coffee sat in front of his angled chair.

He followed her back, turned his chair square to the table, and sat, leaning across so that he was once again much closer to her than was comfortable.

'Like I said, I don't know anything about gardens. So ... have you thought any more about the floors?' he asked, his face losing its sexual appeal as a more serious expression took over.

He might as well have poured a bucket of cold water over her.

She leaned back, tilting her head and lifting her chin defiantly. 'No, I haven't even thought about them this evening. Dave's going to give me a quote—I suppose he'll make recommendations on whether they should come up or not. But seriously, I've been meaning to ask outright, why are you so interested in the floors anyway?'

Grant sat up straighter in his chair, his jaws clenching and unclenching as his head nodded slightly. When he huffed out a few breaths, all her niggling suspicions came together. He knew something.

'Well, I've told you my thoughts. You know, people need to respect history a bit more.' He stood, took his cup to the sink and poured the rest of his coffee out. 'It's terrible the way people want to make everything modern. Tearing down old houses and putting up monstrosities, gutting buildings with character and making them into white-bread versions of their former selves. It's almost criminal.'

She took a sip of her coffee, looking down at the table, afraid to make eye contact and unsure how to respond to this sudden change in his demeanour. The coffee tasted terrible—lukewarm and full of milk. She wanted to get up and toss it down the sink as he'd done, but she didn't want to stand that close to him right now.

He rubbed his jaw, looking at her with flared nostrils, his eyes squinting under his darkened brows. 'It just isn't right. You need to be respectful of the past,' he said, his voice now edging toward menacing.

Flabbergasted by his sudden mood change, it occurred to her it might be best to simply agree with him for the moment. 'Oh, I know what you mean. It has happened in a lot of our older neighbourhoods back home in Melbourne. People used to buy two small houses in a street, knock them down and put up this huge museum-like thing right in the middle of a street where the rest of the homes are simply small cottages. Luckily, most of our councils have gotten smarter, finally, and they aren't issuing permits for that to happen so much.'

His brow creased even further as he stood up taller. He clenched his fists and then relaxed them, intertwining his fingers in front of him so tightly his whole upper body shook. 'I don't care what they do in Australia, you stupid woman. I'm talking about here, in America, in Masons Flat,' he said, his voice having gone up a few decibels.

This whole Dr Jekyll and Mr Hyde thing was scaring her now, and she knew she had to break his train of thought and get him to leave. All she could think of was to go out to the front garden and look at those bare patches up close where, hopefully, he'd get bored and leave.

Trying to appear much calmer than she felt, she left her coffee on the table and gave him a wide berth as she made her way toward the hall. As she reached the door, she turned and called back to him, hoping her voice wouldn't give away her frazzled nerves.

'Grant, come have a look at the garden with me,' she said. She was surprised how normal her voice sounded, but just as she opened the door, he arrived and grabbed her by the forearm and turned her to face him.

His voice was deafeningly loud as he practically spat his words at her. 'I told you I'm not interested in your stupid garden, woman. What I am interested in is your failure to listen to me.'

Her whole body shook as she tried to pull away from him, but her struggle only made him tighten his grip. He was hurting her now, and she could feel tears burning behind her eyes.

'Grant,' she yelled, trying to break through his rage, 'you're hurting my arm.'

She managed to take a step through the door onto the porch, but he came with her, still holding firmly onto her arm.

That's when she spotted Denver racing up the path to the door.

'Grant,' he screamed, 'let go of her. Now.' She'd never seen Denver angry and wouldn't want his anger directed at her.

Grant shook his head as if trying to clear it. 'What the hell are you doing here? Are you spying on us?' he said. His eyes narrowed as he took a step back, releasing his hold on Taylor.

Denver stepped closer. 'I saw your car in the driveway, so yeah, I slowed down as I was driving past, *on my way home*,' he said, emphasising the last bit. 'I had the window down, and could hear you shouting from the street.'

'She won't listen to me,' Grant said, 'she's going to rip up the flooring and destroy that beautiful old building.' The fire had gone from his tone, but his anger was still clearly simmering under the surface.

'She doesn't have to listen to you, or me, or anyone else. It's her building. Give it a rest, man.'

Denver had calmed down, or he was trying to get Grant to calm down. She wasn't certain which it was, but she was certainly grateful he'd arrived when he had.

Grant drew in a loud breath and blew it out with a noisy huff. 'Yeah, all right. I'm going.'

Denver waited until Grant was off the porch and about to get in his car. 'Take the day off tomorrow, bud. I think you need to get some perspective, and being there isn't going to help. Actually, take the rest of the week off,' he said, looking at Taylor.

She nodded, in no hurry to be in Grant's presence again.

'I don't need to take any time off. I'm ... fine,' Grant said as he opened his car door but he didn't get in.

'Take time off anyway. It'll give Jeff free rein to work wherever he needs to work. Then there won't be any patching necessary.'

It was clever, the way Denver made it seem like it was logical in terms of the work. Perhaps he'd dealt with difficult tradesmen on other occasions and knew the right approach to get through to them.

Grant nodded, looking down at the street. His anger had passed, but when he spoke, his voice still sounded edgy. 'Whatever you want, boss,' he said, then got in his car and started it.

Denver watched him until Grant had driven off, then he turned to Taylor.

'Are you okay? Did he hurt you? Seriously, I could hear both of you screaming.'

Taylor rubbed her arm where Grant had squeezed it. 'I'll be fine. Although I'm not certain I would be if you hadn't turned up. I'm not sure what he'd have done next.'

'And that was all because of those stupid floorboards? He's been awfully interested in what you do with them.'

'Yes. Too interested. I think we need to speak to Clay tomorrow. Something about Grant isn't right—and I think maybe Clay needs to look into him, or speak to him, or both.'

Denver reached over gently put his arm around Taylor's shoulders. 'He scared you, didn't he?'

'Bloody hell, he did. It's like he suddenly turned from Dr Jekyll to Mr Hyde, and I seriously can't think of anything I said that would have triggered it. I probably shouldn't have gone out with him again, it's just that ... I think he's hiding something. I wanted another chance to get him talking with a few drinks in him.'

Denver looked at her arm, then bent down and kissed it. 'My Mom used to do that when we were kids ... kiss our boo-boos until they were better,' he said, looking up at her.

Her heart melted at his kindness, and she couldn't help but smile.

He straightened up, released her forearm, and then pulled her into his arms, rubbing her back gently. When she sniffed back a tear of relief, he rubbed a bit harder, and pulled her even closer.

After a time, his arms relaxed, and she leaned back, looking up at him, and when he leaned down and kissed her, it felt the most natural thing in the world.

CHAPTER 24

'Well, you were right about Grant not being completely upfront with you,' Clay said two mornings later when the three of them caught up at the café for a cup of coffee.

Taylor clasped her hands under the table, wondering exactly what sort of man she'd been spending time with.

'Go on, Clay, don't keep us in suspense,' Denver said, taking a bite of his cinnamon bun.

'He's got several thousand dollars in unpaid traffic infringements in Arizona, so I probably could have arrested him, but instead I just threatened to. He sure had a lot to say, though, once I hauled him into the office and told him you were considering laying assault charges.' He turned, facing Taylor. 'How's your arm, by the way? Do you want to make an official charge about it?'

Taylor pushed up the sleeve of her light sweater to reveal the bruise on her forearm. It was already turning an unattractive shade of purple, tinged with yellow. 'My arm is fine ... I don't want to press charges, but I do want to understand what was going on. So he opened up, did he?' she asked, barely able to contain her excitement.

'Did he ever,' Clay said, a smile barely concealed. 'Look, it turns out Grant's father was the butcher at the shop you bought—Don Harrison. Grant goes by his mother's name as his parents never married. Don is in a memory care facility now—suffering from a form of early-onset dementia. Grant is his only next of kin. And over the past year or so, it seems Don has been saying some pretty unusual things.'

'Oh. My. God. Grant's father was Eve's husband?' Excitement charged through Taylor—any wonder he'd driven by their old house and had taken such interest in the bakery.

'Whoa, that's too weird,' Denver said. 'It can't have been a coincidence, could it?'

Taylor turned to Denver for a moment, marvelling at his innocence. Grant's evil intent seemed obvious to her, *now*.

'It was no coincidence,' Clay said, smirking. 'Don's been muttering some strange stuff and it's put Grant on edge. Like, "*she's hidden under the floors*", and "*I thought there'd be more blood*", and "*she just looked like she was sleeping.*" And the statements were all mixed up with lots of laughter and occasional tears. Poor old guy's completely lost it, I guess.'

Denver shook his head. 'Wow, that doesn't sound too good, does it?'

'Not too good at all,' Clay said. 'We're going to send in a forensics team to have a look under the flooring in the butcher shop. They're coming first thing tomorrow so you'll need to tell any workers to take the day off. If the team doesn't find anything there, they'll have a look at the house where the Harrison's lived. Grant said he was never sure which property his father spoke about, but seeing as how the butcher shop's vacant, it's a lot easier to start there.'

'So that's why he came to Masons Flat,' Denver said. 'Now I get it. He must have been watching for the place to sell. Funny, it's been on the market for ages. You'd think he'd have bought it himself and then he could make sure it was never disturbed.'

Clay shook his head. 'He's got outstanding traffic fines, remember? If the guy can't afford to pay those, he definitely wouldn't have been able to come up with the money to buy the shop.'

Taylor huffed out a breath. 'Any wonder he showed interest in me. It had nothing to do with me—it was all about the shop.'

Denver reached under the table and squeezed her leg. When their eyes met, he smiled warmly. 'Oh, I'm sure he was attracted to you, too. Who wouldn't be?'

Clay ignored the exchange and went on. 'When I pressed him about how you were considering charging him with assault he got nervous, so I knew I was onto something. So I pressed harder. Seems the guy has been experimenting with colognes containing pheromones, as in the chemicals that attract women. He's got quite the reputation for being a nuisance at a number of nightclubs there in Arizona. If you found yourself unduly attracted to him, it could be part the reason, although I'm not convinced they are all that effective.'

When Taylor felt her face redden, she looked down to avoid eye contact with Denver. She had been attracted to Grant, but wasn't it simply because he was incredibly good looking, and had been paying her way more attention than she was used to? She looked up at Clay, still not wanting to make eye contact with Denver. 'I've never heard of that ... is it really a thing?'

Clay shrugged, and pursed his lips. Then he picked up his coffee and took a sip. 'Well, like I said, I don't buy it, but who knows ... maybe it has some effect.'

Taylor also took a sip of her coffee, then, wanting to change the subject, asked, 'Am I allowed at the bakery tomorrow, to watch?' Taylor immediately regretted the question. She should have simply turned up rather than risk being told no.

Clay looked at her, raising an eyebrow slightly. 'No one will be allowed *inside* the shop while the team is working.'

~~*~~

After Clay left, Denver took her hand and asked her to walk down to the bakery with him so he could tell Jeff he would have to take the following day off.

From the moment they walked in, the shop felt different. The thought that Eve might be buried under the building made the hairs on her arms stand up. She rubbed them, swallowing back her emotions.

Denver looked completely undaunted, however, and simply told Jeff not to come in the next day. He didn't elaborate as to why.

Jeff caught her eye and nodded. 'Yeah, okay,' he said, turning to Denver. 'But you do want me to finish the work, right?'

'Definitely. It's nothing to do with you. Just a few things that we need to look into before we go any further. I'll give you a call tomorrow and let you know when to come back to finish up. Sorry about the short notice, but it can't be helped.'

Jeff nodded again. 'Should I finish what I'm doing now, or do you want me to leave right away?'

'Finish up when you get to a logical stopping point, and give me a call and I'll come back and lock up,' Denver answered.

Once they'd made their way back to Taylor's car, she turned to Denver. 'We should ring Mark, don't you think?'

'Yeah, of course,' Denver replied, pulling out his phone, setting it to speaker and then making the call.

'I actually just got off the phone with Clay a few minutes ago. It's hard to believe this is happening,' Mark said. 'I believed Don when he said he didn't know where she was, and that the only thing he could think of was she'd run off to be with that cult. What if he killed her, and I never questioned his word?'

Denver's eyes filled with concern. 'We don't know that's what happened, Uncle Mark. I mean, it sounds bad, but the guy's not all there, you know? This could all be something he's imagined, as a way to deal with her running off.'

Taylor looked at him with added respect, again amazed with his skill in dealing with difficult situations.

'No. I'm sure she's dead. I can feel it deep inside. She loved our parents, even if she sometimes disagreed with Dad. That was what didn't sit well with me—her running off and not even keeping in contact with them. I mean, people leave their spouses all the time, but for her to completely disappear ... I should have pushed him to own up to it at the time. I shouldn't have taken him at his word. I should have been a brother, not a friend.'

~~*~~

Taylor stood on the sidewalk outside the bakery with Mark on one side and Denver on the other. They made sure to stay behind the crime scene tape. It was warming up already, and yet she felt cold. She rubbed her bare arms, smoothing down the hairs that kept wanting to stand on end.

Mark stood with his hands clasped in front of him, still as a statue, other than his right thumb which rubbed up and down on his left thumb at the pace of a rabbit's heartbeat.

Denver wore his anxiousness more obviously as he shifted back and forth from one leg to the other, letting out intermittent deep sighs.

Taylor found it stressful, having to wait these final moments to find out the truth. The police had been in there for nearly an hour, and Taylor had felt every minute of the wait. Of course, for Mark, it was the culmination of over thirty years' worth of waiting. She suspected that as much as he wanted this to be over, he was not looking forward to learning the truth.

Although they couldn't see the activity, they could hear it. The police forensics team had lifted the flooring and were now sifting through the earth below.

The street got busier as all the shops began to open, with people driving past on their way to one shop or another. Most drove past slowly, looking over curiously, but no one stopped. Taylor suspected they all knew the outcome of whatever the police were doing would be common knowledge before the end of the day.

When a woman walked up and stood on Mark's left, Taylor leaned forward to see if it was someone she knew. The woman stood nearly as tall as Mark, but Taylor wondered if she would be even half Mark's weight. She wore a scarf wrapped around her head and her face was gaunt, but from the shape of her face and cheekbones, Taylor suspected she'd have been attractive in her younger days. She appeared older than Mark, but it was hard to say for sure. What Taylor was sure of though was that the woman was battling some sort of illness.

'Hello, Mark,' the woman said, her voice surprisingly strong.

He cleared his throat. 'I'm sorry, do I know you?'

'You did. Many years ago. I was Amy Johnson back then. Eve and I were good friends. Being younger than you, you rarely paid us any attention.'

Mark pushed his hands out in front of him, intertwined his fingers, and stretched them out even further as he cocked his head to the side. When he straightened up, he nodded. 'Yes, I think I do remember you. Evie hung out with this girl who looked a lot like her: tall and slender, with long dark hair. Was that you?'

The woman did a mock bow. 'One and the same. Of course, the chemo hasn't done my hair or my muscle-tone any favours, but I've still got my height.'

'I'm sorry,' Mark said, his tone sounding genuine.

'And are these your children all grown up now? I remember them when they were small,' she said, stepping forward and turning towards Taylor and Denver.

Mark shook his head. 'Sorry, I'm so rude. Amy, this is my nephew Denver Gold. And this is Taylor Mason. You might remember Taylor's great-uncle, Steven Mason? He owned the hotel and the saloon as well as a number of the other shops. Taylor's recently bought the old butcher shop and will soon be opening a bakery.'

When the woman nodded slowly, Taylor wondered if she was trying to recall Uncle Steven. 'A bakery? How nice. I remember freshly baked bread as being one of the nicest aromas. Nothing smells good anymore now, after all the chemo. So ... have they run into some problems while doing the renovations?'

Mark cleared his throat, making Taylor wonder if he was going to answer her. It would be all over town by the end of the day anyway so there wasn't much point in hiding it, but it was his call.

Mark finally spoke. 'Yes, well, we think there is something under the flooring. We'll all learn about it soon enough.'

'Oh? Is that so?' Amy said, tilting her head, her facial expression that of a theatre performer's surprise.

Mirroring her body language, Mark tilted his head. 'Yes, that is so.'

The moment Mark finished speaking, Amy's body language changed. She was no longer the surprised theatre performer, but rather a child who knows a secret but isn't sure they're allowed to tell it.

CHAPTER 25

An excited exclamation, followed by raised yet muffled voices, came from inside the shop. Taylor couldn't hear what they were saying, but she had no doubt they'd found something. A moment later, again came the sound raised voices.

Taylor glanced at Mark. His nervousness was palpable. Amy hadn't left. She stood there beside Mark, her face twisted with barely contained emotion. Now Taylor was even more certain the woman knew something.

Finally, Clay came out and stopped in front of them. He stared at Amy, as if wondering if he should ask her to move along before explaining what they'd found. He drew in a few breaths, bobbing his head slightly, deep in thought.

Then he spoke directly to Mark. 'It was a dog. The neck had been broken, as if by a heavy blow.' When he raised his brows and shrugged, Taylor figured he thought the same thing she did. The "she" who Don had been muttering about had been the dog.

When Amy huffed out a rather loud and dramatic breath, they all turned to her. She looked taken aback when she realised they were all staring at her. She stood up straighter, raising a brow and allowing that theatre performer's surprise to reappear. 'What?' she asked, her tone of voice prim and proper.

'I'm sorry,' said Clay, 'I don't think we've met?'

'Oh, I know who you are, Clay Atkins. I watched you growing up. And you should know who I am too if you want to call yourself law enforcement. You'll know me as Amy Whittaker. It was Johnson before that, but I never bothered to change my name back after my cheating husband left town.'

Clay's face softened. 'Oh, I'm sorry Mrs Whittaker. I didn't recognise you at first.'

'Yes, I get that these days.' She rolled her head around dramatically, tapping gingerly at the scarf around her head before lifting an eyebrow knowingly. 'I know who you were looking for ... but you were never going to find her there.'

'Okay,' Clay said, dragging out the word. He said no more but kept watching her.

Mark turned to her, arms crossed close to his body, a frown darkening his face. 'I'm sorry ... who is it you think we're looking for, Amy?'

She shook her head, and made the zipping-the-lips gesture as muffled laughter exploded from her. It was a horrid sound—and instinctively Taylor took a step back. As she did, Denver's arm went around her shoulders, giving her a gentle, comforting squeeze. He, too, must have sensed something wasn't right about how Amy reacted.

Clay pulled out his phone and made a call, speaking a code of some sort to whoever answered. Moments later, two officers, one male and one female, appeared from inside the shop. They stopped on each side of Mrs Whittaker.

The female officer spoke to her in a gentle but firm voice, just loud enough for Taylor to catch every word. 'Is there something you want to share with us, Mrs ...?'

'Whittaker. It's Mrs Whittaker. And why yes, I suppose there might be ... something ... I could enlighten you about.' Amy had composed herself somewhat, no longer laughing but instead looking deadly serious.

Clay nodded to the female officer, who stepped up and placed her hand on Amy's arm. Then he turned to face Amy. 'How about you go with the two officers, Mrs Whittaker, and have a little chat back at the office?'

CHAPTER 26

1985 – Eve

I turned my head slightly, reaching around to tug the strap of my purse back up onto my shoulder. As my head turned, I caught a glimpse of movement further along the porch. A second later, a figure emerged from the shadows. Dressed in dark clothing with a hoodie, it was impossible to see his features, but it had to be Don. My heart thumped. Why would he stand out here in the dark? Why hadn't he gone into the house to wait for me to come home?

'Hey, what are you—' I asked as I turned to face him.

The movement was so quick that if I'd blinked, I'd have missed it. What I didn't miss was the most severe pain I'd ever felt at the back of my head, followed by blissful nothingness as I felt myself drift off into unconsciousness.

~~*~~

At first, I had no idea where I was or what was causing me so much pain. Everything hurt, and I wished I could go back to the glorious state of sleep from which I'd just woken.

I was lying on my back, and something sharp stabbed me where I guessed my kidneys would be. My leg hurt so much I knew it had to be broken. I tried to shift to ease some of the pain but I couldn't get my hands to my sides to push myself up. That's when my brain recognised the numbing pain in my hands and wrists.

Up until this moment, there was a possibility I'd simply fallen off the porch and landed awkwardly in the garden. Now, as the fog in my brain cleared, I wriggled my fingers and felt scratchy rope around my wrists. My hands were definitely bound.

Had I been struck and then tied up and dumped somewhere?

Fear drenched me like a bucket of cold water, distracting me from my pain. My heart raced as though I'd run a marathon and my stomach clenched and churned.

Had I been abducted? Was it a burglar rather than Don who'd been on my porch? Had he knocked me out and tied me up so I couldn't ring for help?

The darkness made it impossible for me to get any sense of where I was. All I knew was that it was cold and damp, and the strong smell of rotting vegetation made my stomach churn. I suddenly felt the overwhelming need to vomit. I tried to roll to my side but couldn't move. At least I was able to turn my head to the side, although even that hurt like a son-of-a-gun.

The sound of me vomiting and coughing afterwards must have caught the attention of whoever had done this to me. But why would they still be here? Surely, if they were robbing the house, it wouldn't take long. There wasn't much there to steal.

'Enjoying your rest?' a muffled voice called out a moment later. It was impossible to tell from which direction it had come.

I tried to focus my eyes and then realised something else. I was blindfolded—any wonder it seemed so dark. I reached up with my bound hands, surprised I could do so, and tried to pull at the blindfold, but I couldn't get a grip on the material. My fingers were so numb it was useless.

'Hello?' I tried to call back, but my mouth and throat were thick with bile from my vomiting—it came out as more of a croak. I coughed, trying to clear my throat, and tried again. 'Hello? Who's there?'

A round of screeching laughter met me in reply. Then I heard another sound—a hollow scraping sound.

'Hello? I ... I can't move. I think I might have broken my leg. Can you help me, please?'

The only reply was more laughter, followed by the hollow scraping sound again.

The hope I'd felt when I discovered I wasn't alone disappeared as the source of the sound dawned on me. It was metal on rock. Whoever was out there had a shovel. Warmth between my legs told me one of two things had happened: either my water had broken and my baby was coming way too early, or fear had caused me to urinate. I hoped, with every ounce of my being, that it was the latter.

'Please, I'm pregnant. I need medical help.'

'You need to shut your mouth,' the voice called down.

Down.

Yes, the voice was coming from above me.

Perhaps I'd been thrown down into a hole of some sort. An abandoned mineshaft? Or a disused well? I tried to turn my body so I could touch the sides of whatever hell-hole I was in, but I couldn't roll. Had I broken more than my leg in the fall?

'Please, don't do this. I'm begging you. Please ... think of my baby if not me. Please.'

'I told yer to shut your trap, and I wasn't kidding. Shut it, or you're gonna get a mouthful of dirt,' the voice said again. This time the voice sounded female. A moment later, a shower of dirt and rock fell onto me.

Too late, I did as she'd said, and for my delay, I got a mouthful of soil. I turned my head and spat out as much of it as I could.

The metal on rock sound came again, followed by another shower of dirt, this time containing larger rocks. One hit me square in the temple. I wondered how many times this could happen before I'd be knocked unconscious? If I was going to die, I hoped the black oblivion would return quickly.

I had to try to reason with my captor, but how? Panic brought the lie to my lips.

'I have money. I can get a hold of lots of money. Of course, you'll need to help me get out of here for me to do that.'

For a moment, the sound of the shovelling stopped, and I allowed myself another faint moment of hope. I wasn't sure how I could get my hands on money, but I would face that problem later.

Suddenly pain erupted as a sharp object struck me on the right side of my face. I'm certain I could feel blood trickling down my neck.

'I said shut up, and I meant it you cheating bitch. You and your bastard don't deserve him. I knew he'd left you. The moment I walked by the butcher shop and saw he wasn't there. Don's never missed a day of work since he opened the shop. He left you because you're not good enough for him.'

Realisation struck me with as much force as that rock had. It had to be Amy. No one else knew I'd cheated. No one else could possibly know a child I was carrying could be a bastard. Amy, whose husband had left her, and who was the one person I'd stupidly confided in. She'd said she'd had a crush on Don during high school. In some deranged way, did she think by killing me she was doing him a favour? Or did she think that with me out of the picture, she could finally have Don to herself?

I had to try to get through to her. 'Amy? I know it's you, Amy. Please, listen to me. We can sort this out. We can talk it through. I'll leave town. And I won't tell anyone about this ... not any of this.'

Another rock flew down on me, this time hitting the other side of my face. The throbbing pain energised me and my mind started to spin, searching for a different approach to take.

A moment later came that dreadful sound of the shovel followed by another shower of dirt and rock. I tried to turn my head, but dirt still got in my mouth and some into my nose. I coughed, hard, expelling as much of it as I could.

When silence followed, I again allowed myself to hope she was having second thoughts. Then I heard a grunt, followed by her screeching voice calling out, 'Take that, you bitch.'

Something hit me, heavy and hard. The pain was intense, but only for a brief moment. Blackness enveloped me once again as I drifted off into nothingness.

CHAPTER 27

Present Day

'Who was that woman?' Taylor asked, turning to Mark after the two officers had escorted Mrs Whittaker toward their car, and Clay had excused himself to go back inside to talk to the forensics team.

'Amy Whittaker. She and Evie were good friends in school but, to be honest, I don't remember Evie ever talking about her after they graduated. I think they went their separate ways—Evie left town to go to college, and Amy stayed here and got married.'

Taylor nodded, thinking of her own school friends with whom she'd failed to keep in touch. 'She seemed a bit odd, don't you think? But she sure hinted about knowing something. Do you think it's possible?'

Mark shook his head. 'I have no idea. I haven't seen her for years—not since we moved to Sacramento anyway, and I don't remember seeing much of her even when we did live here. But Clay clearly thinks she might know something or they wouldn't have taken her away to talk to her.'

As Taylor leaned closer to Denver, his arm tightened around her shoulders. The goose-bumps she'd felt when she'd first walked into the bakery, after hearing what Grant had said about someone possibly being under the floorboards, returned. She rubbed her hands up and down her bare forearms.

A moment later, Clay reappeared. 'They'll wrap up in there over the next hour or so. Once they finish up, it's all yours again—you can get back to the work you were doing. Oh, and sorry about the floors,' he said, facing Taylor.

'So will they go to the house where Don and Evelyn lived now?' Mark asked, jiggling his hands in his pants pockets nervously.

Clay frowned thoughtfully. 'I think we'll wait to see what this Mrs Whittaker has to say first. She may just be attention seeking, but until we find out for sure, I see no point tearing up someone's house.'

'That makes sense. I guess there's nothing more I can do around here today. I'll wait to hear from you, Clay.' Mark said.

'We'll be in touch as soon as there's anything to tell you. I'm heading to the office now, to see how they're going with Mrs Whittaker. Denver, Taylor, we'll talk soon.'

With that, Clay left, and Mark said goodbye and headed in the opposite direction to his car.

Taylor leaned closer into Denver. 'You realise if I hadn't bought this shop, that metal box would still be sitting on the ground under there, and Eve would still be considered a missing person who'd run off to be with a cult, right?'

Denver gave her a squeeze, pulling her tight to his body. 'I sure do. Who knows when another buyer might have come along? The building was on the market for years. And even if it did sell, there's nothing to say they'd have found that box under the floorboards, or that they'd have cared about it if they had found it. And if the building had been demolished, for example, the little box might well have been carted off with the rest of the rubble to a dump somewhere.'

Taylor sighed—torn between a sense of gratitude about finding the box and anxiety as to the whereabouts of its owner. 'I imagine you have a lot to catch up on today? Seeing as how standing here probably wasn't on your list of things to get done.'

'Yeah, I've gotta get back to work. Are you okay? Do you need company? You're welcome to follow me back to my place and roll up your sleeves. We can always use a bit of help cleaning out stables.' He winked, and the gesture made her smile.

'Thanks for the offer, but I think I'll go see if I can coax Alex into taking off early and spending the afternoon with me. Might even go for lunch somewhere new—just to get away from here for a bit.'

Denver leaned down, planted a kiss on her forehead, and gave her another squeeze. 'Talk soon?'

'You bet,' she replied, doing her best to look far more relaxed than she felt.

CHAPTER 28

1985 – Amy

Amy sat in her car, her head positioned so she could see the door of the butcher shop without it appearing obvious she was watching it. Each time a customer went in, she waited for them to leave, but every time she started to get out of the car, another would turn up.

It had been over two weeks since the incident with Eve. Two weeks of waiting. Two weeks of not knowing who might have seen Eve's car that night or who might have suspicions as to where Eve had actually gone. Two weeks of waiting for the sheriff to turn up on her doorstep, asking about her whereabouts on the night Eve had last been seen.

But no one had come knocking on her door. No one had even looked askance at her as she'd gone about her business in town over the following days. Perhaps the rain that had come only a few hours after she'd driven off with Eve's car, and hadn't stopped for nearly twenty-four hours, had done enough to cover any and all evidence of the car and cycle tracks. Perhaps luck, for once, had been on her side.

Rumour had it that Eve had run off to be with some sort of cult or something. Absurd, of course, but so long as it drew suspicion away from foul play, there was no way Amy would do or say anything to slow its spread.

She'd wanted to see Don right away. To see how he was taking the absence of his wife. Would he be sad, or was he relieved the cheating tramp had skipped town? Would Don think Eve had run off to be with her lover? Did he even know Eve had cheated on him? Surely, he'd have doubts about where she'd gone. Surely, the rumour about her going off to join a cult was just a cover-up he'd devised to take suspicion away from himself?

As much as she'd wanted to see Don, she'd held off—biding her time, pretending everything was as it had always been—wanting the first time she saw him to be nothing out of the ordinary.

Now, sitting in her car, Amy's thoughts crept back to that fateful night. She hadn't meant to kill Eve, had she? Wasn't her original intent merely to scare her away? She let out a tiny laugh. Who was she trying to kid?

Remembering Eve's croaky voice as she'd begged for her life, remembering looking down upon her shadowy figure sprawled awkwardly at the bottom of the shaft. Eve had claimed to be pregnant. Of course, that might have been nothing more than a last-ditch attempt to gain sympathy—trying everything in her power to get her captive to release her.

But what if it was true? What if Eve had actually been pregnant?

Amy tried to recall the last time she'd seen Eve at the shop. Could she have been pregnant? Had her face glowed the way a pregnant woman's often did? Had she worn looser clothing to hide a growing waistline?

No. Eve hadn't seemed any different than usual. It had simply been a tactic to try to gain sympathy.

She cast all doubt away and watched as the last woman who'd gone into the butcher shop left with a large parcel. Looking up and down the street, she could see no one heading for the shop. Hopefully, they'd be uninterrupted for at least a few minutes.

It was now or never.

She got out of her car, methodically locked the door behind her, and slowly made her way across the road. It was hard to walk calmly when every nerve ending in her body screamed with impatience.

'Ah, Mrs Whittaker, how are you today?' Don asked as she entered the shop. His tone sounded pleasant. Was he happy to see her?

'Good, thank you, but please, call me Amy. I'm hardly a Mrs anymore.' She hoped it sounded light-hearted rather than desperate. It had been ages since there was a Mr Whittaker on the scene, and for the first time since he'd left, she regretted not changing back to her maiden name.

'Yes, of course. Amy. And what can I get you today?'

Hearing him say her name was intoxicating and she struggled not to imagine him saying it under more intimate circumstances. And although both his voice and words were simply professional, she was certain she'd detected a slight smile in his eyes.

She stared into the display filled with slabs of meat and swallowed hard, willing herself to say what she'd practiced all morning. When they finally came out, they were a bit rushed, breathless. 'Well, I thought I might do a pot roast—not a huge one, but enough for me to have a couple of meals. Of course, I could get a slightly larger piece of meat ...' She paused, hoping to make it seem as if she'd just gotten the idea. 'I don't suppose you're getting home-cooked meals at the moment. Would you like to join me for dinner?'

She took a step back and looked up at him, trying to appear shy. She was anything but shy, but he wouldn't know that. He'd only had eyes for Eve in all the years she'd known him.

Don cleared his throat and sort of bobbed his head as a frown developed on his brow. 'That's very kind of you, Amy, but under the circumstances, I don't think I'd feel comfortable with it. I mean, I expect Eve ... well, she could come back any day now and of course I'd like to be home when she does. So ... I think I'll have to pass on your very kind offer.'

Oh, it's only a meal, for God's sake. She nearly said the words out loud but caught herself in the nick of time. 'Oh, well, if you think it's inappropriate, by all means. I only thought you must be a bit lonely and missing coming home to the smell of a roast in the oven.'

Don stood taller, and his eyes narrowed briefly before he buried whatever emotions were charging through him and returned to his professional retailer demeanour. 'As I said, it's a kind offer, but one I can't accept. Now, what can I get you?'

Heat raced to Amy's cheeks as rejection engulfed her. She fought the desire to fling self-defensive insults at him, knowing that would be counter-productive. This was her fault. She'd approached him too soon.

She turned and looked out the window momentarily as she gathered every strand of her often-disobedient self-control, then turned back to him and flashed a warm smile. 'Well then, enough for me to do a small pot roast then, please.'

Back in the car, she sat grinding her teeth, angry that she'd let her impatience get the better of her judgement. She should have waited another few weeks. Or a few months even. Time was on her side, after all. It wasn't like Eve was going to come back and get between them. Not this time. No, she would wait. And next time, she would be successful. She would get him, in the end. She had to. Otherwise, this would have all been for nothing.

CHAPTER 29

Present Day

Several days had passed since the forensics team had torn up the flooring at the bakery—days during which Taylor had continued to oscillate between gratitude, at being able to press on with the bakery works, and anxiety, due to the ongoing mystery surrounding Eve's disappearance.

Thankfully, Grant left town shortly after Clay advised him that Taylor wasn't going to press charges for the assault. Denver received a text message from Grant, asking for any wages he was entitled to be deposited directly into his account, and then neither she nor Denver had seen or heard from him since.

Taylor had seen Denver every day, though, if for nothing else so he could give her a brief update on progress at the bakery. They'd also shared a meal at the hotel a few times. And one night, they played pool at the saloon. Keeping busy had helped, but whenever she wasn't busy, Taylor's mind grappled with all the possible outcomes of the mystery of Eve.

And then Denver got a call from Mark.

Eve was dead. They'd found her remains.

Mark told Denver he didn't know if he'd be able to recount all the details correctly, and that it would be better for them to meet directly with Clay.

Although it sounded plausible, Taylor suspected it had more to do with Mark not yet being ready to talk about Eve's death so objectively. In some ways, she was glad. It gave her more time to come to terms with it herself.

This afternoon, as Taylor walked into the saloon, she spotted Denver at a table in the corner, far enough away to be out of earshot of the two other patrons standing at the bar chatting to Darleen.

Denver jumped up when he spotted Taylor and walked over to greet her with a quick kiss on the cheek. They sat, and a few minutes later, Clay walked in.

After drinks were arranged, Clay got right to the point. 'If I'm repeating things you already know, feel free to hurry me along.'

'Mark told me you found her, but nothing more,' Denver replied, looking to Taylor for support. 'He was pretty shook-up about it, so I felt it best to wait to hear all the details from you.'

When Taylor drew in a long breath and nodded, Denver turned to Clay again. 'Uncle Mark now knows he should have done more to try to find her right from the start. Not that it would have changed anything, but ... you know.'

Clay took a long draught of his beer and then set the glass down on the table. It appeared he was trying to work out where to start. 'It's never easy—not even after thirty-odd years.'

He made eye contact with Taylor first, and then Denver. 'Mrs Whittaker is not a well woman. Apparently, she's been told she has less than a year to live, and she wanted to come clean before she dies. Makes you wonder, you know, how much of her illness could have been caused by carrying around such a terrible secret for so many years.'

Taylor had been aware the discovery was related to the interview with Mrs Whittaker, but hearing it confirmed sent shivers down her spine. She crossed her arms, rubbing at the goose-bumps on her bare forearms as she recalled the appearance of the gaunt woman.

Clay caught her eye again and when she nodded, he continued. 'Mrs Whittaker took her time coming clean with it all, mind you. But my colleagues don't give up easily, especially when they think a witness is concealing some of the truth. She finally spilled everything on their third interview.'

He paused, just long enough to take another drink of his beer. Taylor glanced at Denver, whose fidgeting suggested he was as anxious as she was to hear the details.

'It seems Mrs Harrison had confided in Mrs Whittaker about her extramarital affair, and Mrs Whittaker was deeply upset by the knowledge. She'd been in love with Mr Harrison herself and never believed her friend deserved him, so when she heard about the affair, it triggered some terrible thoughts. She said she stewed over the whole thing for quite some time, getting angrier by the day. My guess is she started planning to do something and then waited for the right opportunity to arise, and then wham,' he said, hitting his fist on the table.

When Taylor jumped back, Clay shook his head. 'Sorry, I shouldn't have done that.' He dropped his voice and gave her an apologetic look.

Denver reached over and threw his arm around Taylor's shoulders, giving her a gentle rub. 'Are you okay?'

She nodded. 'It just startled me. Go on.'

Clay cleared his throat and continued. 'Yeah, again, I am sorry about that. So anyway, when she figured out that Mr Harrison was out of town, because he hadn't turned up at the butcher shop and his truck was nowhere to be seen, Mrs Whittaker lay in wait for Mrs Harrison to come home, abducted her and made it look like she'd run off.'

'And it worked,' Denver said, still rubbing Taylor's shoulder. 'All this time, Uncle Mark assumed she'd gone off with a cult. Or at least that she'd gone off with them to start with, anyway.'

Clay cocked his head, thinking again. 'Based on what your uncle said, I'm pretty sure Mr Harrison really did think she'd run off. Of course, knowing what we now know about the affair, it's possible he knew about it as well, and if so, that he'd assumed she'd run off to be with the man. I suppose it would have helped him save face in town, saying he suspected she'd run off to be with a cult rather than that he'd been cheated on.'

'So you think he found out about the affair?' Taylor asked.

'It's hard to be sure, but from what I ascertained, it was out of character for him to be away from town mid-week like he was, so my guess is he might have gone off to think things through. Unfortunately, that was what gave Mrs Whittaker the opportunity to abduct Mrs Harrison.'

'What does Don, Mr Harrison, say about it? Have you spoken to him?' Denver asked.

'Not personally. He's been told, but it's questionable as to how much he's taken in. He's not terribly lucid, so it's hard to say whether he even understands what's happened.'

'And so, Mrs Whittaker ... she confessed and told you the whole thing?' Taylor asked, finding it hard to understand how a woman could do that sort of thing—especially to someone who'd been a friend.

Clay nodded. 'She claims she only went there to scare Mrs Harrison, but we have our doubts.'

He paused, frowning, then continued, speaking slowly.

'She rode her bike to the property and hid in the bushes until Mrs Harrison got home from work. Then she snuck up on Mrs Harrison, whacked her with a baseball bat, tied her up and threw her onto the backseat of Mrs Harrison's car. She spotted a small suitcase in the kitchen, grabbed it and then, using Mrs Harrison's keys she locked the door behind her. Then she threw her bike into the trunk and drove to the furthest corner of her property and dropped Mrs Harrison into an abandoned mineshaft. The whole story sounds far too organised to be anything other than pre-meditated.'

Taylor cringed as the details of how Eve died hit home. Denver pulled her closer, his hand gently rubbing her shoulder.

'Are you okay? Shall I continue?' Clay asked.

Taylor nodded, afraid that if she tried to speak it would come out as a weak croak.

'When she was certain Mrs Harrison was dead, she parked the car in her barn and covered it with old sheets and dried up hay. And then, it seems, went about life as though it had never happened.'

Taylor looked at Denver, shaking her head. He appeared as stunned by the revelation as she was. It was unimaginable. When she turned back to Clay, he continued.

'When the team got to the site, it didn't take them long to find the shaft. It had a rusty barbed-wire fence all around the perimeter and was covered with blackberry bushes, but she'd given them good instructions on where to find it. But if Mrs Whittaker hadn't said anything, I'm not certain Mrs Harrison's body would have ever been found.'

Finally, Taylor found her voice. 'But it was on Mrs Whittaker's property, right? So when she dies, the property will be sold. Maybe she figured Eve's body would be discovered at that stage anyway, or at least her car would have been, right? Perhaps she just figured she might as well have it discovered now,' Taylor said, wondering if it gave Mrs Whittaker pleasure knowing that soon the whole town would be talking about what she'd done.

'No, she'd burned the car years ago,' Clay said. 'Seems she realised she should destroy it a few days after the incident, so she drove the car out into one of the pastures and set fire to it. The team found the burnt-out body but, after thirty-odd years of being out in the weather, there wasn't much left of it. Forensics should be able to confirm it was Mrs Harrison's, knowing what we already know, but would anyone have even cared about a burnt-out old car body if she hadn't confessed? I think not. And as for the mineshaft, they're pretty unstable, so a new owner might have simply chosen to dump a load of dirt and rock into it, and maybe even cement, to save stock getting injured if they got through the fence.'

There was silence for a moment as both she and Denver seemed to be digesting Clay's words.

'It must have been tricky getting her out,' Denver eventually said. 'As kids, remember how much trouble we got in that time we found an old shaft and decided we had to investigate it?'

A wry smile touched Clay's lips as he shook his head. 'I couldn't sit for two days; I got such a hiding.'

'So, how did they get her out then?' Denver asked.

Taylor wasn't certain she wanted to hear all the gory details of how they retrieved Eve's remains, and yet her curiosity got the better of her. She had to listen to the answer.

'Those things are notorious for having rotting timbers and unstable rock formations. Kids get stuck in them from time to time, which is why my dad was so furious. So, to answer your question Denver, carefully, that's how. They built a frame over the top and sent a team member down on a rope with a pulley. He took a ton of photos first, and then loaded her remains and all her belongings onto a sling, and they pulled her up.'

'And there was no doubt about her identity? They're certain the body was Evelyn Harrison—in the shaft?' Taylor asked, still not wanting it to be true.

'There's no doubt. They're in the process of checking dental records, as a matter of course, but it was pretty clear. For one thing, there was her purse. It had her driver's licence and a few other identifying cards in it. And then there was her wedding ring—still on her finger. It matches the one in the wedding photos her brother supplied. And there was also the vinyl suitcase. Even after all this time, the personal items inside were in relatively good condition.'

'So Mrs Whittaker was thorough, taking a suitcase of belongings the way she did,' Taylor said. 'But of course, she'd have had no idea about the box hidden under the floor at the butcher shop.'

'No, she clearly had no idea about that,' Clay said, rubbing his fingers along his jaw slowly.

A chill ran down Taylor's spine at the thought of being at the bottom of a dark shaft, unable to get out, just lying there waiting to die. Then she had the thought that perhaps the drop had killed her. Would they know if it had, from examining her remains?

'Do they think ... I mean, is there any way to tell if she was still alive when she was dropped down there?' she asked, her voice scratchy with emotion.

'I couldn't say. There was quite a bit of damage to her skull so it's quite possible the initial blow killed her, or even if it didn't, she might not have regained consciousness,' Clay answered, his voice remaining steady. 'A baseball bat can do an awful lot of damage.'

Taylor thought about that. Yes, she must have been knocked out, at a minimum. If she'd struggled, it was hard to imagine Mrs Whittaker would have been able to get her there. She'd said she'd been an athlete, but still, carrying a struggling woman her own size was hard to imagine.

She looked up to find Clay staring at her, the atmosphere between them thick with unsaid words.

'There's something else, isn't there?' she finally asked.

Clay nodded. 'Yes. There's one more thing. The report is only preliminary, but they're fairly certain about it ... it seems Mrs Harrison had been pregnant.'

Taylor swallowed hard, but the lump growing in her throat made it nearly impossible. She sniffed and looked down at the table. Amy Whittaker had killed two people that night: Evelyn Harrison and her unborn child. Would the child have been Don's, or would he or she have been Andrew's? Would they do DNA testing to find out? What purpose would even be served by knowing?

~~*~~

After Clay left, Taylor stayed at the table while Denver went up to the bar, bought two shots of whisky, and carried them back.

'To Eve,' he said, raising his glass.

'To Eve,' she said, touching her glass to his. 'May she finally rest in peace.'

They downed the shots, set their glasses on the table, and sat staring at each other for a moment.

'How about we go for a little walk to clear our heads? It's a gorgeous afternoon,' Denver said, standing.

Taylor nodded, and followed him out the door.

As they headed left down the street, the air was quite warm, and there wasn't even the slightest breeze, and yet when they passed the church at the end of the street, Taylor felt a slight shiver run down her spine. She swallowed hard, wondering again about Eve and the child she was carrying and what they might have achieved had they both lived.

She tried to pull herself back to the present as they continued through a residential area. Taylor hadn't walked this far out of the township in this direction and as she focussed on the lovely homes, she was pleasantly surprised by them. When they eventually came to a creek, with a wooden bridge over it, they made their way to the middle of the bridge and then stopped.

Taylor again felt a shiver run down her spine as she wondered if this might have been somewhere Eve used to come.

'Nick and I used to come here after school sometimes when we were kids,' Denver said. 'We had these old fishing poles, and we'd catch worms on the bank over there and then sit here for hours, hoping something would bite.'

She smiled, grateful the image of the two young boys took away thoughts of Eve. 'I take it nothing ever did?'

Denver blew out a breath. 'No, but it didn't matter. It was just a way for us to sit and talk.'

'You were close, I take it?'

'Pretty close. We're the same age, you see. Travis is seven years older than me, so we didn't see much of each other at school, and by the time I was a budding teenager in need of someone to discuss the worries of the world with, he'd gone off to college. So Nick and I talked.'

'That would have been nice. I always had Casey. Alex was older too, but when she went off with her tennis career, Casey and I talked about everything.'

Denver reached over and took her hand, giving it a squeeze. 'You know you can talk to me about anything, don't you?'

She stared into his eyes, and it was like she saw them, really saw them, for the first time. 'Yes, I do know that. Thank you, for being here ... for being you.'

He released her hand and then turned to face her. He reached up and ran the back of his fingers down her cheek as a smile touched his lips. When he spoke, his voice was soft, soothing. 'I will always be here for you, Taylor. Always. No matter what. I mean, I'm pretty sure everything that was going on with you and Grant was his fault, and besides, it's history now, but even so ... if you're not sure about how you feel about us, I can wait. I will wait.'

Tears welled in her eyes. Denver was the most genuine man she'd ever met, in every sense of the word. And she did love him, but what still had her baffled was whether the love would last forever. How did people know? And if she didn't know, how could she possibly deserve him?

'Oh Denver, I never loved Grant—not the way I love you.' Her hand flew to her mouth. She hadn't intended to say that.

His eyes softened, glistening. 'You love me? Could it be possible? Because if you do, I will never let you go, and I'll do my best to make sure no one ever hurts you again.'

She swallowed hard, biting her lower lip, struggling with tears that threatened to spill. Her emotions were raw from learning about Eve, and she felt completely exposed and unprepared for this discussion. When she tried to speak, nothing came out, but it didn't matter because Denver took her in his arms and held her so tight, she could barely breathe. There was no need for words.

'Look, we don't have to talk about this right now. It's been a rough week. I'm sure both our nerves are a bit raw.'

She pulled back and looked into his eyes. And when she did, she knew.

Without any doubt or hesitation.

Of course she loved Denver. She'd loved him from the first time he'd smiled at her, from when they'd played pool together—him in his cast, barely able to stand—from when he'd taken that first bite of her pumpkin pie and the look on his face had made her insides go all warm. Her love for him had grown slowly, getting stronger each time she'd seen him.

Their love wasn't based on the crazy chemistry Casey always spoke of—it wasn't like the rush she'd felt with Grant that had turned out to be all smoke and mirrors.

Their love was something so much more. It encompassed respect, and compassion, and understanding, and kindness. Its foundations were built upon common goals and interests and morals and integrity.

Denver was the man she'd always dreamt of marrying one day. She'd let doubt creep in because it felt too contrived—two brothers with two sisters, and then their other sister with the men's cousin. She hadn't believed it could possibly be real.

But why not?

She reached up, putting her arms around his neck, and then closed her eyes as she leaned forward to give him a gentle kiss. When she pulled back and opened her eyes, every shred of doubt vanished.

'I do love you, Denver Gold. More than I ever thought possible. I'm so sorry about what happened with Grant. You ... you deserved better.'

He shook his head, smiling, his eyes glistening even more than they had been. 'Shush now, Taylor, that's history. And in some ways, I'm glad Grant came along. His presence helped me see how much you mean to me. We belong together ... you know that, don't you?'

Warmth penetrated her to the tips of her toes. 'I do, Denver Gold, I think I've always known it, I simply didn't trust it was real.'

EPILOGUE

The mid-day September sun shone warmly, and only a few fluffy clouds broke up the cobalt blue sky as the small group stood beside Eve's grave, listening to the pastor begin the service.

Denver was to her left, and Travis and Alex stood on her right. Casey and Nick stood at the foot of the grave.

Directly across from her, on the other side of the grave, were Mark and his wife, Linda. Beside them, closer to the foot of the grave, their daughter Stacey stood beside her husband and daughter.

This afternoon, it was just the family.

With one notable exception.

A tall, dark-skinned man stood beside Mark, nearest to the pastor. He was lean, in an athletic way, his greying hair the only suggestion that he was not a young man. He wore a dark, expensive-looking suit and sunglasses. The only colour on his person was the two yellow roses he held gently in front of him.

He hadn't attended the memorial at the church where the town's residents had gone to pay their respects, instead arriving moments before the pastor commenced the graveside service. Taylor suspected everyone in the group knew it was Andrew Fletcher.

A light breeze teased the short tendrils of Taylor's hair, escapees from her knotted updo. She reached up to push them aside as she dabbed at her eyes with a damp tissue. She hadn't even known Eve, but it didn't make her loss any less poignant. Two weeks had passed since they'd made the discovery, and yet she still found herself shedding a tear from time to time. Denver must have seen her dab at her eyes, as the moment her hand went back to her side, his own hand wrapped around it, giving it a gentle squeeze.

When the pastor finished his initial words, he gestured for Mark to speak. Mark told stories of what it had been like to have the kindest sister in the world—one who'd been smarter than the rest of the family put together and whose laugh could make even the sourest old man smile. Taylor marvelled at his strength as Mark delivered his words; not a prepared speech, just words spoken from the heart.

When Mark finished, the pastor said a few last words.

'With thanksgiving for the life lived, and the love shared, we commit the remains of Evelyn Harrison and her unborn child to the ground, earth to earth, ashes to ashes, dust to dust, knowing that what was special about Evelyn lives on in our hearts and in the eternal realm of a God whose love is stronger than death.'

When he finished, a bagpipe began to play the heart-wrenching strains of Amazing Grace as Mark, Travis, Denver, and Nick slowly lowered the casket into the grave.

As the final echo of the bagpipe faded, Andrew leaned forward and said something to the pastor, who nodded. Then Andrew tossed the roses into the grave. Taylor could see his lips moving as he said something she suspected no one could hear—final words to the woman he'd loved. As he stepped back, Taylor could tell he was trying hard to hide his pain—pain no doubt exponential in comparison to her own.

When the ceremony finished and everyone began speaking in hushed tones, Andrew turned and headed toward the car park.

Excusing herself from Denver, Taylor was beside him in a few quick strides.

'Andrew, I'm so glad you were able to make it.'

He stopped walking and turned to her, clearing his throat before he spoke. 'Taylor. I should have known it was you.' When he took off his sunglasses and smiled, a pair of the most beautiful grey-green eyes met hers. She understood in a heartbeat why Eve had been drawn to him. She suspected that most days his green eyes completed his youthful appearance. Today, however, they were red-rimmed and bloodshot.

Movement at the edge of her peripheral vision caught her attention. She turned as Denver stepped up, putting out his hand. 'Andrew?'

Andrew took his hand. 'Yes, and you must be Denver? Taylor's told me the role you played, bringing in your friend to investigate Eve's disappearance.'

Denver nodded. 'It was at Taylor's insistence. It was just lucky I knew someone to contact.'

Andrew released Denver's hand and stood looking from one to the other of them for a moment, and then he looked down, speaking softly.

'Not knowing was the worst. I tried to convince myself she simply couldn't continue to see me. That she'd put me out of her mind and was working on her marriage. I had always hoped that's what it was ... which is why I kept up the letters. I couldn't give up hope that she might write, or might come to me if her situation changed.'

Taylor swallowed hard, her throat tight with emotion. 'I knew she wouldn't have gone to a cult. She wouldn't have left your letter and photo behind. And the trinkets that had to have been so special. It just didn't make sense. I had to know the truth.'

'Women's intuition is a powerful force. Eve and I talked about such things. We connected on so many levels. I ...' he stopped and drew in another deep breath, 'I never married, you know. I've had relationships, of course, but I held out hope that one day Eve and I would find each other again. I did try to look for her, but it wasn't easy back then. It wasn't like now, with social media and online directories and ways to track people down.'

'No, I struggle to imagine how different life was before we all had twenty-four-seven access to the internet,' Taylor said.

Andrew nodded as he put his sunglasses back on. Taylor took it as a signal that he was about to leave.

He cleared his throat. 'Thank you for giving me the details for the service. I needed to come ... for closure. I'll never forget her, you know, and I won't stop wondering what might have been if I'd succeeded in talking her into coming with me. But at least ... maybe I can move on now. I can try, at least.'

A slight breeze once again caught a tendril of Taylor's hair. When she went to tuck it back behind her ear, she had the strangest sensation—as though someone else's fingers were brushing the wisps of hair away from her face.

She looked at Denver, but he was still facing Andrew. Then she allowed her gaze to focus back on Andrew.

He appeared different now, younger. His hair appeared darker, without the smattering of grey. And his whole aura seemed lighter, as though he, too, had finally found some sort of peace.

She blinked slowly, and in the second that it took to blink the mirage, which had momentarily wiped away the years from Andrew's countenance, faded.

'Don't be a stranger, Andrew. I mean, if you're ever in the area, and want to drop in for a home-cooked meal and a glass of locally produced wine, we would love to have you at our table any time. Or better yet, stay for a few days. I've put off opening the bakery until after the funeral, but I'm having a grand opening on the weekend. Are you able to stay?'

Andrew sniffed, nodding slowly. 'I would like that, Taylor, but I have commitments. I'd have enjoyed seeing a bit more of the town, however, particularly the bakery. Can we make it another time?'

'You'd be welcome any time. If I know you're coming, I'll make a special treat for you, and you can sit in Eve's corner.'

'Eve's corner?' he asked, his frown visible even with his sunglasses.

'Yes. My sister is helping me—she's quite the artist. She'll paint an impressionistic version of Eve's trinket box, and the items it contained. We'll have two small tables for the occasional patron to sit with a coffee and a cake, and we'll put up a sign saying Eve's Corner. Seems appropriate, don't you think?'

The smile on his face said it all—he was touched and overcome with emotion. He gave her a quick nod before glancing toward the parking area.

She reached over and gently placed her hand on his forearm. 'Oh, and speaking of the box, and its contents ... can I send them to you? Would you like to keep them? It makes more sense than me having them.'

He looked back at Taylor and swallowed hard, and even through his sunglasses Taylor was certain he was squinting back tears. He cleared his throat. 'You hang onto them for now ... for safekeeping. It'll give me a reason to come back here.'

Taylor nodded, finding it hard to control her own emotions.

Andrew looked back toward the cars, nodded again, and said a soft goodbye.

She watched for a moment as he strode away, then she turned to face Denver.

'That was very kind of you, Taylor, inviting him to drop in sometime. He seems a nice man ... someone I'd have liked to call Uncle Andrew, you know?'

'Yes, I do know,' she said, reaching for Denver's hand and giving it a squeeze. 'Shall we?' she said, gesturing back toward the gravesite where the others were still mingling, no doubt sharing memories.

~*~ THANK YOU ~*~

Thank you for taking the time to read this third and final book in the Romancing the Californian Cowboys series. If you've enjoyed this book, please consider leaving a review on Amazon or Goodreads as this helps other readers to find the book.

If you enjoyed the series, you may also like to look at my other series, the *Copperhead Creek Australian Romance* series, which is set in the sleepy rural town of Willows, Australia.

The fictitious town of Willows is located in Victoria's Golden Triangle, the home of Australia's 1850s Gold Rush, and is inspired by small towns scattered throughout Victoria and South Australia. Each book can be read as a stand-alone featuring a new couple who find their own happy ending, but if you read the books in order you'll find characters from earlier books making reappearances as the lives of the small town residents overlap and tangle.

The books in the Copperhead Creek Australian Romance series are:

Taking a Chance (a FREE series prequel)
A Chance to Come True
A Chance to Get it Right
A Chance to Let Go
A Chance to Belong
A Chance for Snow
Murder at the Creek – A Copperhead Creek Mystery

~*~ ABOUT S M SPENCER ~*~

S M Spencer grew up in the San Francisco Bay Area where she rode horses along the beaches and across the tops of the rolling coastal hills of California. In the 1980s she was offered a job in Australia, which was the beginning of an adventure of which she has never tired. Still living in Australia, she writes from the semi-rural home she shares with her husband, horses, cats and dogs, as well as the kangaroos that pass through the paddocks from time to time.

You can find all of S M Spencer's books by visiting S M Spencer's Author Page at Amazon:
https://www.amazon.com/S-M-Spencer/e/B00PGE0G9U/

And never miss a new book, or a promotion, by following S M Spencer's blog: http://smspencer.online/blog/

www.ingramcontent.com/pod-product-compliance
Lightning Source LLC
LaVergne TN
LVHW090941080826
845145LV00003B/842

* 9 7 8 1 9 2 2 2 7 0 7 0 2 *